How to Travel Incognito

VOLUME III IN A NEW

H James H. Heineman   New York   1992

How to Travel Incognito

BEMELMANS SERIES

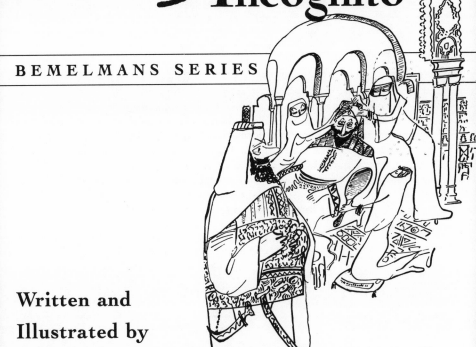

Written and
Illustrated by
Ludwig Bemelmans

H

James H. Heineman, Inc.,
475 Park Avenue,
New York, NY 10022

To

Armand de la Rochefoucault

*Who said to me one evening
as we sat in a small tavern
which is called th
Little Nest of St. Cucuface,
and which is located in the
Forest of St. Cloud,
outside of Paris:
"Why don't you write
something amusing, to cheer up
the sorry world."*

Contents

How to
Travel
Incognito

1.

In a First-Class Compartment

IN THE first-class compartment of the train from Blois to Paris, sitting next to the window and facing the direction in which it was going, was an American woman, a tourist, a refugee from a conducted tour of the Châteaux de la Loire. She dismissed the historic safari with the words: "Nothing but thick walls and running comment." Opposite her and pressed into the corner sat a man in deep sleep. He had pulled the curtain forward and the air was whipping it back and forth. He was tall, and had immense hands which were folded in his lap over the top of a cane. The conductor entered our compartment and punched

3

my ticket and that of the lady tourist; he carefully did not disturb the sleeping passenger and when he left he very quietly closed the door. The man reminded me of a marsh bird such as I had seen in Flanders, for even in his sleep he seemed conscious of the length of his legs, and had stretched one diagonally into the corner, the other was thrown over it and relaxed. He wore elegant and polished boots, but appeared to have no socks on his feet. His suit was the color of a marsh bird's egg, a dark green speckle on an earth-brown ground, with black lines woven irregularly into the material.

In a land of individuals, he stood out even in his sleep. He was apparently without luggage.

The train was several kilometers out of Blois, when the dining-room steward entered and whispered that he had places left if anyone wished to go to the second sitting. The man in the corner continued peacefully sleeping, the American woman shook her head and suddenly, to my astonishment, burst into tears. She was a nice-looking woman of about forty, as could be seen by the reflection of her face in the window. When I asked her if there was anything I could do, she said, "No, thank you." A moment later, staring at the landscape, she said apologetically: "That always sets me back, the mere mention of food. That's why I finally left him, all on account of a steak. It just seems that he can't be happy unless he is making somebody else unhappy. We went to this château and that château; he always wants to do everything in a systematic way like his stamp collection—he cared more for that stamp collection of his than he even did for me. I tell you, if he knew there was a two-cent stamp lying in Central Park somewhere, he'd grab his hat and run out for it.

4

"Well, anyway, we stayed overnight in this hotel that was a château. Nothing was the way he liked it, and that poor manager—he's going to have the manager fired—he always writes letters to the management and tries to have everybody fired. Well, I looked in the mirror yesterday morning and I took the hairpins out of my mouth and I said to myself: 'I've had enough.' I just packed up and left, and you know, last night I had the first good night's sleep since I married him. And I bought myself a hat, this hat, the first hat that I bought for myself in fourteen years. I bought it in Blois. And it started to rain, and a man, the nicest man, offered me his umbrella. He spoke English with a cleft palate and complimented me on the new hat. I could hardly understand him but it made me feel real good." I looked at the telegraph poles slanting past. "I should have known better," she said. "The day before we got married, he says to me: 'I like Schrafft's.'

"So there we are in Schrafft's and he orders a steak and he tells the lady captain just exactly how he wants it done. I order the chef's salad. When the steak comes, he looks at it; he sniffs at it like a dog and then he snaps his fingers at the lady captain.

"'I want to see the manager,' he says, 'immediately.'

"'Yes, sir.'

"She goes and gets a man. 'Ready for the complaint,' he says.

"'Are you the manager here?' he says.

"'No, I'm the assistant manager.'

"'Then go away and get me the manager of this place.'

"'I'm very sorry, sir, but the manager has just stepped out. Is there something I can do for you?'

"'Stepped out at the peak of business?'

"'Well, to tell you the truth, sir, he has been absent for some

5

time; he is indisposed, sir; he is at home in bed. Is there anything I can do, sir?'

"'Well, yes. You can get me one of those small boxes that you people put your cupcakes into.'

"'Yes, sir.'

"'And then you can bring me some wax paper.'

"'Yes, sir—anything else, sir?'

"'No, that's all.'

"Well, when the assistant manager brings the stuff to the table, my husband wraps up the steak in the wax paper—and mind you there wasn't a thing wrong with it—and he says to the poor man:

"'You know what I am going to do now? I'm going to the Hotel Pierre, to the thirty-second floor, where the owner of this restaurant lives'—he always seems to know things like that—'and I'm going to walk right in and show him this and ask him to explain to me how it is possible that an inedible piece of meat like this is put in front of a customer at Schrafft's.'

"So the poor man starts to beg:

"'Oh, please sir, don't do that. Please excuse us, sir. Please let us get you another steak.'

"Well, I couldn't stand it any longer and I took the box and I told him what I thought of him. He got another steak and ate it, and I moved to another table so that people wouldn't think I was with him. Well, something just like that happened day before yesterday in Blois, when we went to visit the castle. Thank God, I'll never have to look at another castle in my life; that's another thing that makes me feel just dandy.

"You take a castle like Blois, with all those empty rooms you

6

have to walk through. So because he speaks French, we have a French guide who speaks so fast that I only get a word now and then like Renaissance—and 'Glorious pages of our history,' which he said every few rooms. Well, we had a longer tour than anybody. Phil—that's my husband—kept asking a lot of questions. This happened with every door, picture, chimney, and tapestry. So when we're finally through the castle, the guide says that by the grace of God none of the churches in Blois were destroyed, so we have to visit them. And then, the guide says that religious architecture, interesting as it is, cannot rival the civilian edifices of Blois, and so we have to visit the house of Pierre du Blois, and the Hôtel Sardini. I thought we might get something to eat at the Hôtel Sardini, but I found out that '*Hôtel*' can mean a private house in France as well as a regular hotel, and from there we go to the house of Robert the Magnificent. As we come out of the last house he says, 'We have just time to visit the museum'—so we go to the museum and by that time I am dead on my feet and hungry. The guide knows a good restaurant, he says, and next to this was the place. There were a lot of tourists and a waiter came with a menu, on it is a picture of Brillat-Sarvarin the Great Gourmet." She laughed bitterly at this point of her story, and explained, "Phil taught me to appreciate life. The waiter recommended all the specialties of the house: a hot goose-liver paste with raisins, and then a pork sausage cooked in carrot soup. Phil made a face at the goose-liver and the pork sausage, and when the next dish came he got real mad, and called the waiter, and barked at him. But these Frenchmen are not like the people at Schrafft's. Phil asked for the proprietor. So the chef comes out of the kitchen and makes a terrible row. So Phil says he doesn't want to talk to the cook, he wants the proprietor, so the chef tells him that he is the proprietor. He called Phil a lot of names, and then ordered him out of the restaurant. He even followed us halfway up the street with quite a crowd following. Phil was stunned; he wouldn't go to another place, so we just quietly walked home and we had some tea at the hotel. After a while he began to complain. I guess he thought he could take it out on me. Well, I had heard the last complaint I was going to listen to, and for once I yelled right back at him, just like the chef. You should have seen the surprise on his face, when the worm finally turned."

All during this recital, the man opposite had slept peacefully without changing position. When the train stopped, however, he came to life with great suddenness. I had an old umbrella which got in his way and he stepped on it, breaking the ferrule. He seemed not to have noticed it and was out of the car in a great hurry, running with long, springy steps until he disappeared in the crowd of people heading for the exit.

The lady liberated from the château country and Phil said, "You know where I'm going now? I'm going to the American Express Company—he always hated it—he said it was only for tourists. Well, that's where I am going. I'll let them get me a room, and the next ship home, an American ship, I don't care if I have to travel steerage."

In many ways Paris is a large village. A week later, I saw her again in the Place de la Concorde. She still wore her liberty hat, but I was introduced to Phil, who, it seems, had traced her through the American Express Company. They were on their way to the Louvre.

Cocktail Party

I have said that Paris is a village. I encountered the man who had sat opposite me on the train at a cocktail party at the Hôtel Georges V given by a steamship company to inaugurate a new service and to encourage tourist traffic in general. He stood at the end of a long buffet, which was piled high with food, munching quietly and sipping from a glass of champagne. He was attired in a blue suit and a pair of tan and white shoes. I noticed that his shoestrings were untied. His stomach sagged and his shoulders were pushed forward, he turned his head, and suddenly smiled and waved with a sandwich in my direction. Since he had been asleep during the voyage from Blois to Paris, I was astounded that he should appear to recognize me and greet me as though we were old acquaintances.

He put down his glass and came over to me and again I was struck by his resemblance to an agitated bird. He was no longer stooped, and his walk was a series of birdlike hopping movements and sudden stops. The skin of his face was a transparent green, and there was a constellation of black moles on his left cheek. He commented on the rigors of inspecting châteaux and on the woman who had shared our compartment. "You know, I had a sleepless night on her account," he said. "I kept thinking about her story. I felt so sorry for that assistant manager in the American restaurant. One always thinks of Americans as Millionaires, Gangsters, Cowboys or Detectives — men of action — at any rate not as poor wretches like the assistant manager in Schrafft's."

"But I thought you were asleep," I said.

10

He offered me a cigarette from a large ivory case with a crown on its cover.

"There is a way of traveling cheaply in France," he said. "One simply gets on a train, sits down in a first-class compartment, and falls asleep. There is a law in France that no first-class passenger asleep may be awakened by a conductor. They may awaken you in second or third class, but never in first. Considering that we are a republic we have more regard for privilege than any other nation on earth." He took a glass dish from the buffet and offered me crackers with *pâté de foie gras*. He ate four of them very rapidly and held out his glass to be replenished by the waiter. He drank thirstily and continued: "There are other ways, but they are more difficult. For example, it is possible for two to travel on only one ticket. In this case, you simply wait for the approach of the conductor, and then you disappear with your friend into the washroom. As the conductor knocks, you open the door a little and hand him the one ticket to punch."

He introduced himself as the Count of St. Cucuface.

"This salad," he said, pointing at a bowl, "is what?"

"Chicken salad, Monsieur le Comte," said the butler. Cucuface took a silver spatula and put some on a plate and turned to eat it. He disposed of it with astonishing speed.

"There's St. Cucuface," said a man nearby to a woman in black velvet with a sparkle of diamonds at her ears, throat, wrists and shoes. "He's one of the authentic antiques of France. Poor chap, he is now reduced to living off cocktail parties. He's the legs of the buffet; without him the table would fall down at that end. He's the first to come and the last to go."

Pushing people out of his way, advancing like a snow plow through the white summer dresses of the pretty young girls, a heavy man, jovial and self-assured in the company of his equals, bowing, and occasionally lifting a pudgy hand in greeting, moved toward the buffet, and, lifting the covers of the various chafing dishes, announced sadly that he was on a diet. He wandered toward the spot where St. Cucuface was inspecting a good-sized roast turkey. The bird was held by the fangs of a silver rack, and had been sliced into slabs, convenient to pick up and eat. The fat man took three slices of turkey and rolled them up. The turkey roll disappeared in one swallow, and immediately he started on another. St. Cucuface observed him with interest and proceeded to imitate him.

It was the time of plenty again. *Vogue* photographed fashion in Paris. *Life* photographed life in Cannes. The beautiful people were back in Paris, but some of them were still dissatisfied. The fat man munched steadily and then said to the woman in black velvet and diamonds:

"I'm going to open a hotel in Paris. A real hotel. The first thing I'm going to do is get some Canadian telephone operators, bilingual, you know, and trained to talk to you like human beings; not like these yapping old biddies you have to listen to now. Maybe you haven't done much telephoning, but over here the operators do the talking and you do the listening. Yes sir, we'll have good telephone service, and you'll also be able to get real shoeshines. I'll get some Italians for that. Look at my shoes—" He held out a foot. "You know, it's impossible to get a decent shoeshine in France. And we won't have any of this lousy French cooking—I want some good American coffee, and dishes like you'd order at home: real toast, ham and eggs. Do you know that in this whole damn country, from the Atlantic to the Mediterranean, you can't get a decent plate of ham and eggs? In fact, there is a conspiracy against breakfast. The other day I went into a place in Nice and asked for a half grapefruit for breakfast. Well, would you believe it, they served it to me, for breakfast, with liquor on it—they had doused it with Kirsch. Now, in our hotel you'll get a good American breakfast. And no tourists. You'll meet the right people. We'll have to be careful; it's for the rich of course—and by rich I mean rich. In July and August we might have to let the bars down and let in some bums; but for the rest of the time, it'll be just us."

"We're dining at eight at the Princess Stucci's. Come on, dear," said a voice. The fat man turned his back on St. Cucuface and moved away from the turkey of which now only the carcass was left.

St. Cucuface came to me and pulling out his cigarette case, said: "You will give me three thousand francs for this, no?" The franc had been stabilized. Three thousand francs was about ten dollars and I gave him the money. He expressed a wish to see me again and asked for my address.

"You are very fortunate," said a thin Austrian baron. "That is a sign that he likes you and has confidence in you. Cucu doesn't sell his cigarette case to just anybody."

I went home. At that time I lived in an old hotel in a most romantic setting and difficult of approach: the Hôtel St. Julien le Pauvre, on the Left Bank near the church of that same name. It was another authentic antique of France. The ancient silk of the curtains tore when one touched them, chairs occasionally collapsed as one sat down, the mattresses seemed to be stuffed with cabbages and the circular stairs sagged so badly that one could overcome the pull of gravity only by leaning at an angle to them in the fashion of the motorcycle daredevils who negotiate

perpendicular walls at county fairs. This hotel *de grand confort* had been my home for years before the war. There is nothing in the whole of America to compare with it; the only such place of old-world charm and discomfort that I have known was the old Bartholdy Inn, an actors' hangout near Times Square which burned down around 1920. The prices of the St. Julien le Pauvre, however, are absolutely first class.

A week after the cocktail party, St. Cucuface called on me. A little self-consciously, he announced that he had received an offer of fifteen thousand francs for the cigarette case he had sold

14

me for three thousand, and he was sure, he said, that I would be happy to return it to him. "We will arrange the details later," he said, putting the cigarette case back in his coat pocket. From the courtyard of the hotel came the sound of dishes and the smell of cooking. Apparently there was no cocktail party that day, and St. Cucuface looked hungry; I asked him to dine with me: he accepted at once, saying, "I hope I can be of use to you."

About Servants, and How to Dine Cheaply in France

The agility of the French mind in conjuring up appetizing names for eating places is remarkable. There is the Agile Rabbit, the Chope Danton, the Mediterranée, the Porquerolle, the Crémaillère, the Auberge de Fruit Défendu, the Coq Hardi. There are ten thousand restaurants of various categories in Paris serving every sort of appetite, nationality and pocketbook. Restaurants for diabetics alone number more than a hundred and one of them is even named "Insulin." Besides that, every week someone discovers a new place, better than all the others. I had in one of my pockets a slip of paper with the address of the latest discovery and after I had found it, I wanted to call and reserve a table. Like all things in France, my telephone was an instrument of great personality. One could never bunch conversations; there had always to be pauses. St. Cucuface had just hung up after making a call, and therefore I had to wait for several minutes.

There was always a humming noise when you took off the receiver, the sound of a mosquito hovering near your ear, clear and insistent as on hot summer nights. This was followed by a

barrage of rapid noises, rather like the assault of a flotilla of outboard motorboats racing, after which would come a click and then the voices of either of two operators. These ladies I could have drawn both in profile and in full face, simply from hearing their voices. One, a telephone functionary old in service, absolute and obstreperous and with all melody gone from her voice, with a bun of black hair on the back of her head; the other also a veteran of similar format and age, but giving off a few, faint vibrations. In her, the woman was not altogether dead, it flickered only briefly, like the last reflected sunlight in one of the many windows of a large factory: a flash of light and then only the dead dusty panes again. It was the second one, the occasionally illuminated operator, who answered as I took the phone off its hook.

I gave the number of the restaurant and after a while I got it. I said I wanted to reserve a table.

"For whom?"

"For Monsieur Bemelmans—"

"Will you spell it please?"

In France, B is *boe*, e is *oe*—

"*Boe—oe, em, oe*— No no no—*Boe*—as in *boeuf*—"

The telephone girl at the restaurant was apparently also temperamental, for she said, "Never mind, Monsieur, don't disturb yourself, we haven't any tables left," and hung up.

Since in most French restaurants, of this type, the telephone girl and coatroom woman are one and the same and usually either the wife, relative or a former mistress of the proprietor, there is little use in asking for the owner. Over the hum of the phone, I could hear the voices of the place and then the sound of the outboard motors and the hum of the mosquito. I hung up and as we were debating where to go, the phone rang, and the unexpected, that always happens in France, happened. It was my operator number two, who said she had called the restaurant back and spelled my name for them and had also delivered

herself of a few opinions on the treatment of tourists in Paris and that the table was now properly engaged and awaiting us.

The elaborate pleasantries which are necessary to properly express gratitude for such service above and beyond the call of duty are endless. The lamplighter had done the entire square in front of St. Julien le Pauvre when at last all the various compliments and expressions of gratitude were exhausted.

"Now where is this wonderful place?" asked St. Cucuface. I gave him the slip of paper but on it was only the telephone number. I had forgotten the name of the place. So there was the problem of making another call. Since we had just finished a lengthy conversation over the telephone it required a rest, and after a second cooling-off period the address of the new restaurant was finally obtained.

As we walked down the circular stairway, St. Cucuface said: "You know, you have all the attributes of the perfect tourist: patience, meekness, persistence, endurance and most important of all, perpetual curiosity. I can almost guarantee that from the way this has begun that we are going to spend an uncomfortable evening." Few things are more difficult to bear than the responsibility for another's well-being. We sat silently in the cab, and Cucuface referred again to the matter of the assistant manager at Schrafft's in New York:

"I had no idea that anything like that existed in America. At least I never came across it when I was there. In fact, I found quite the opposite: the cowboy, the gangster spirit. I was at the time very fond of a lady who had invited me to her place on Long Island. She had a butler. In America I suffer your difficulties with my name—here in France St. Cucuface is not unusual. It is an old and distinguished name; there are hundreds of us: dukes, princes, marquises and counts. In America the name Cucuface makes people laugh. The hostess naturally called me Cucu and so did everybody who came to the house. The only person who had some regard for me was that butler.

"'Count,' he said to me, 'you don't know what a pleasure it is to serve you. I am so sick of these bastards.' He supervised my valet, who was also very friendly, as he unpacked my bags. I had a bungalow with a pantry with an icebox and in the icebox there was always a ham, a roast chicken, caviar, champagne, beer, milk, soda and potato salad. In the living room was a bar stocked with whiskey and gin so that I could entertain. The formal dinner was of course served at the big house. The butler complained a great deal. He spent more time in my bungalow than at the house and once I said to him, 'You don't have to answer me—but what do you get paid?' 'Oh,' he said, 'not really enough for all the trouble I have. She pays me two hundred and fifty dollars a month and a few extras.' 'What do you mean by extras?' 'Oh, I have a house, and she sends my children to school, and here and there something like a station wagon or some other gift, and she always remembers the wife's and the kids' birthdays.'

"Just before I left, he came again. 'Count, may I take all this junk?' He meant the ham, the chicken that was always there, the champagne and caviar and the liquor. 'Certainly you may,' I told him. He put it all into a hamper and went off with it in the direction of his house.

"He must have stolen thousands of dollars' worth of things a year. The hostess had no conception of the value of things. There was a robbery in her house while I was there, but she never reported it. Her husband had a horror of reporters and of publicity. Anyone could have taken anything at that house. But to go back to servants—

"A few months later in New York I had another bad experience. A friend invited me to dinner at his house. He had told me only the week before what a magnificent cook he had. At the last minute he called and said that instead of dining at his house, we would go to a restaurant in New York called the Pavillon. When I met him there his wife said, 'Forgive us, but our servants decided to leave. We had invited two other people we wanted you to meet, and we had forgotten to tell the cook in

time; that is, we told her at five. So she and the butler, the
kitchenmaid and the valet all left.' Just then our waiter came to
the table jingling some car keys. He gave them to my friend
saying, 'Your chauffeur sent these. He has left the car outside.'
He had resigned also.

"So we ate a very good dinner and I thought of my good
Salvatore, my Italian servant, to whom I have sometimes given
my socks at midnight to wash for the next day, saying: 'Here,
wash them and darn them so I can put them on tomorrow.' And
he will smile and say, 'Certainly, quickly.' He refers to *our* house,
our garden, and to my three shirts as 'our laundry.' In the
country I pay him three dollars a month and when I don't have
the three dollars he will not ask for them until he knows I can
spare them. I am like his father. My God, that butler in Long
Island, he lived more like a prince than I ever did."

With the aid of a policeman and a little boy who ran beside
the cab, we finally arrived at the restaurant. The place was
crowded and the headwaiter had a list of reservations. He tilted
his head and I went into the spelling game again. His pencil
moved up and down the row of names written on the back of a
menu and he shook his head. We suffered the stares of several
attendants and of the coatroom girl. I finally asked for the
proprietor and told him that I was a great friend of so-and-so
and of others and that the place had been recommended to me
by a famous gourmet. He listened with some sympathy and
surveyed the room, and then he motioned us to the lobby. We
sat down near the swinging door that led out into a dirty
corridor and after about half an hour we followed a bill of fare
held aloft by the headwaiter and were shown to a table far in the

back and so small that as we sat down our knees bumped together.

"Do you mind?" said Cucuface, as he arose. "My poor friend, you must never allow them to do that to you again. Let's get out of here." We got up; Cucuface stopped in the foyer and offered me a cigarette from the beautiful ivory case. "Do you always live like this?" he asked in a tone of compassion, putting an immense hand on my shoulder.

The proprietor, suffering from an automatic reflex, had pulled a match from a box and lighted my cigarette.

"I never eat anywhere where I am not properly received," said Cucuface, taking a light himself.

"Is there anything wrong, Messieurs?" asked the proprietor anxiously.

"Where is the telephone?" asked Cucuface ominously. The telephone was a few feet away attached to a gilded column. St. Cucuface snapped his fingers for the page who attended to the opening and closing of the inner door of the establishment.

"*Chasseur,*" he said to him or rather to a spot several feet above the proprietor's head, "get me Maxim's." He made it sound as though he had said "Get me the police."

When the famous restaurant answered, he said in a voice loud enough for the proprietor to hear: "Albert, a table for two for the Prince de Bavière."

The proprietor laid a trembling hand on the arm of Cucuface and summoned the headwaiter. "You head of veal," he shouted, and turning to Cucuface he began to implore him: "Monsieur le Prince, one moment please." Cucuface said, pointing to me,

22

"That is the Prince, I am merely the Marquis de St. Cucuface."
He demanded his hat, cane and gloves; the coatroom girl stood
with a deck of stubs in her hand and looked helplessly at the
proprietor; the page boy barred the door. "Come, my dear
friend," said Cucuface to me.

"Mon Prince, Monsieur le Marquis," pleaded the proprietor,
holding both hands up before St. Cucuface's chest, and then
bowing, "do not, I beg you, make me suffer for the stupidity of
my employees—allow me—"

The coatroom girl had mirrored the various emotions of the
owner of the place.

Finally Cucuface allowed himself to be persuaded. The proprietor guided us to a freshly laid table in the best possible
position. He begged to be allowed to order the dinner. "Certainly," said Cucuface graciously. "All but the wine." He proceeded to examine the wine card carefully, and the wine waiter
and the chastened maître d'hôtel exchanged glances of ap-
proval at the selection the Marquis was pleased to make. The
menu was superb, the wine was all the name and the year
promised and the oldest brandy was served in thin, large,
warmed inhalers. It was all exactly as it was supposed to be and
so seldom is.

"Allow me," said St. Cucuface as he asked for the bill. The
proprietor came running again. He begged, "Monsieur le
Prince, Monsieur le Marquis, I beg you, do not make me suffer
further. It is all my pleasure. There is no bill."

Cucuface now reached for his wallet, an extremely thin,
worn and empty looking envelope of black leather also deco-

rated with a crown. Again the proprietor protested, "Please, it is all taken care of. I hope you have enjoyed your dinner. Is there anything else you desire?"

"Yes," said St. Cucuface. "I have a dog, and I wonder if I might have a small bone for him?"

"Ah, but certainly," said the proprietor. He ran out into the kitchen and came back with a plate of roast-beef bones and some meat, which he wrapped in a menu and tied with a string.

We departed through an aisle of bowing waiters.

"I hope I have been of some use to you," said St. Cucuface to me. "I felt I owed you a dinner."

2.

How to Be a Prince

INSTALLED in the best hotel in Paris, the one that faces the Place Vendôme, I paid less than I had at the Hôtel St. Julien le Pauvre, because of a reduction of one third the normal price. This is a courtesy extended to diplomats and visiting royalty.

It was a rainy month, and my umbrella needed some minor repairs. I went out to find an umbrella shop, but at each one I found myself treated with indifference. The people in charge simply shrugged their shoulders. In one of them, on the Avenue de l'Opéra, the proprietor explained that all the men who did

25

such work had either vanished or died. "We are in the machine age, Monsieur. Buy a new one," he advised me.

I went to meet St. Cucuface for lunch at a restaurant which deserves the most sincere recommendation. It is called the Chope Danton and is located at the Carrefour de l'Odéon. The first time one goes there, the impulse is to walk on, for it makes no pretensions whatever. The exterior is discouraging, and the interior banal. It has a tiled floor, the usual twisted stair which only one person at a time can ascend, and two tired waitresses who resemble the room and who sag like its tired chairs. The food is excellent, though, and the proprietor is that rarest of persons among restaurateurs: an honest man and a connoisseur of wine, who buys his good bottles at the place of their origin, takes care of them himself, and sells his wine at a fair price. When we were seated, St. Cucuface said:

"You must take full advantage of your title. You are now no longer a tourist to be pushed about. You are the one to do the pushing. You will give bad tips and be better served than anyone else. You must not pay your bills and shopkeepers will therefore swear that you are indeed a real prince. Hasn't your telephone service improved since you have become the Prince de Bavière?" I said that it had.

"I decided on 'Prince de Bavière,'" he said, "because it goes with 'Ludwig.' And of course there was once a mad King Ludwig of Bavaria. I have also chosen it because it goes well with your beery physiognomy and the *gemütlichem* accent. Now, how does it work?"

"Miraculously," I said. "I have not once had to spell my name."

26

We ordered *escargots* and a steak with pepper; and by that I do not mean green or red peppers, but a small steak put in a pan and cooked with roughly ground, ordinary black peppercorns, and served with watercress. The owner tenderly carried the bottle of *Hospice de Beaune* in a basket in his arms, and held the basket carefully against the wall so that the bottle would not be shaken as he pulled the cork.

"Perhaps we will never again drink such wine," said St. Cucuface when he had tasted it.

The wine was so good we decided to return and finish the six bottles the proprietor had informed us were still left. The price was one dollar and seventy-five cents a quart.

"What did you do this morning?" asked St. Cucuface.

"I tried to get my umbrella repaired; the one you stepped on as you rushed out of the train that day. I must have gone to a dozen shops, but nobody seemed to know how to fix it."

"What is wrong with it?" asked St. Cucuface.

"The small piece that sticks out at the end—the ferrule—is broken off."

"And what did they say?"

"Nothing. Just that they couldn't fix it."

"Did you tell them who you were?"

"Nobody asked me."

"Tomorrow," said St. Cucuface, "I will bring you an umbrella with which everything possible is wrong. And I guarantee you, that in the first shop you enter, they will fix it."

"Why?" I asked.

"By the simple device of 'Prince,' fat accent, face and all. You don't know what a lost race of royalists the French are, particularly makers of umbrellas and canes. They are closely related to the makers of swords and armor, to the designers of heraldry . . .

"I have a broken umbrella that will delight their hearts. It is the Napoleon-blue silk umbrella of my grandfather, the Duke of St. Cucuface. The peaceful looking armament of my ancestor . . . An heirloom. In France, umbrellas are handed down through generations like jewels. One of the last things my Grandfather Louis did with it was to break it over my head. The handle flew off, and a golden band on which is inscribed a martial Latin epigram.

"I had been most carefully educated by him to become as magnificent as himself. Although Mistinguett was by that time already fifty, and tradespeople were received in society, he brooded months over his dinner invitations. He lived in such splendor that he was known in his own circle as Louis Quatorze St. Cucuface. He was truly the snob of the world.

"I tell you, it is a terrible thing to be in the hands of servants, especially the devoted ones, bless their dear old cotton socks. And I was, and I could have murdered them all. The moment I became of age and came into some money, I took a ship for America in order to get as far away from the châteaux of my family as possible. I stayed a whole year before I returned from my first voyage to the United States. And then I had the greatest nostalgia for that country that anyone can suffer. I admired everything American, and since I had inherited some money from one of the several hundreds of Cucuface aunts, I decided to do something American with it. It was at that time my dream to be a businessman.

"One of the men whom I admired most in America was the

28

razor king, a Mr. Gillette, whose face appeared on the wrappers of every one of the millions of blades he sold.

"I looked through the gallery of portraits of my ancestors and found a painting in my grandfather's house of a very early one, the Duke Philippe de St. Cucuface. He had the most regal of Cucuface features. I employed an artist to make a design from it, giving him as a model the wrapper of the Gillette blade. He incorporated all the various elements very skillfully into a blue folder on which I had printed, in gold, 'The St. Cucuface Blade.'

"I proceeded to outdo the Americans in industry. I had an office, a desk, telephones, a cable address and a secretary. I drank milk and ate crackers for lunch. I ordered the advertising, and had the blade enlarged into a poster and I plastered Paris with it. I even had enormous packages made, in facsimile, inside of which sandwich men walked, with only their feet showing, and they looked out through the eyes of the Duke's picture on the package. I drove all night with the first pack of blades to the castle. I had sent a telegram ahead and when I proudly entered, they were waiting for me.

"It was like having the decorations torn from your uniform. All of them had assembled. They stood in the great stairhall and it was there that my grandfather broke the umbrella over my head, and not only banished but disinherited me. They went further and took me to the courts. My office was closed, the company became bankrupt, and I went back to having lunch at Maxim's.

"So much for the history of the umbrella," he concluded sadly.

He sighed and reached for his cigarette case.

We had coffee and brandy. The proprietor was honored, impressed and grateful that his esteemed client had brought a royal personage to his humble restaurant. He said that his best wines would be reserved for us always, and it could have again been a free lunch. But the integrity that occasionally burdened St. Cucuface got the better of him. He asked for the bill.

Before leaving, St. Cucuface made an appointment with me for the next day. He also made a wager that the owner of the first shop we walked into — and I had my choice of any umbrella emporium or parasol factory in France — would be beside himself with happiness at the opportunity to repair the umbrella.

He arrived at the appointed hour the next day dressed as for a duel: long black coat, dark gray gloves, opera hat; and he carried the case which contained the umbrella under his arm as if it contained the pistols.

"If you like," he began, "I am willing to bet a hundred dollars that the cost of repairing the umbrella will not be more than two thousand francs."

I said that I thought the bet we had made for five thousand francs, that they would repair it at all, was sufficient.

"You don't trust me, *mon Prince,*" he said sadly. "I may appear to be irresponsible, but when it comes to betting I have the most rigid code possible. I will deposit with Georges at the Ritz bar one hundred dollars in travelers' checks—"

"Show me the umbrella," I said.

"Not before you agree."

He opened the rotting leather case. Its contents resembled the bones and feathers of a long-dead bird, one tropically beautiful.

He turned the aged, yellow ivory handle, decorated with the St. Cucuface crest. It revealed itself as a snuff-box. The tiny golden hinges on which it opened were broken; the golden ring with the martial epigram dangled loosely from a sword blade as St. Cucuface took the handle out of the case.

"Sword canes are no great rarity," he explained. "But of sword umbrellas, this is the only one in existence."

The silk hung from the whalebone frame like an antique battle flag. The ribs refused to open.

"Come," said Cucuface, putting the sword umbrella back into the case.

We walked around the Place Vendôme. Jewelers and furriers, Schiaparelli and the Ministry of Justice have their offices there; there is also a hat shop and a men's furnishing establishment, but no cane or umbrella shop. In the Rue de Castiglione there is Meyrowitz the optician, several bookshops, the Hotel

Lotti, and Sulka's shirt-and-tie store, but no parasol shop.
There is a gendarme always at the intersection of the Rues St.
Honoré and Castiglione, and we approached him.

"Monsieur l'Agent, where can one have an umbrella repaired?" asked St. Cucuface.

"Ah . . ." He looked hopelessly up into the sky and then down
into the Rue St. Honoré, and the Rue de Castiglione, and then
his mind began to function. He asked a passing girl.

"*Parapluie, mais oui,*" she said, and pointed down St. Honoré
to the left, where the church is. "At the church, you turn right,
you see it, an umbrella hangs outside."

"*Merci,* Mademoiselle; *merci,* Monsieur l'Agent."

"Now," said St. Cucuface, who had begun worrying about his investment, "I will tell you how to do it. It is very simple." He rehearsed me briefly in the behavior of a prince who has a broken umbrella to be fixed.

We followed the girl's directions and soon came to a store on the outside of which hung a red metal umbrella. In the store window stood an assortment of canes: snakeskin, Malacca, blackthorn, with ivory handles and gold bands. At the right of these was a group of ladies' umbrellas and sunshades, both gay and serious, some with handles set with semiprecious stones and carved into the likeness of birds and animals, and some with handles covered with the skins of various lizards and snakes. The men's umbrellas, all of them of black cloth and dedicated to hard use, formed two rows, stuck into holders leaning away from the wall. On the window was lettered *Parapluie* and on the door *Entrez*.

I took the doorhandle and opened the door. "Dingaling ding ding," sounded the ring of a bell. We entered the store.

A bitter little woman in black, with pince-nez whose chain ended in a golden capsule attached to her right shoulder, faced me behind a counter.

I stood for a while surveying the establishment. Then I said, simply, "I am the Prince of Bavaria," and smiled with condescension while St. Cucuface ceremoniously put the case on the counter and retired to the wall. I took off my gloves and said nothing. The formula worked instantly. The little lady smiled and inspected the battered case.

As I opened the case, the lid fell off and the curiosity of the proprietress increased. Her hands were held out toward the broken umbrella.

"Of all the items in my collection of umbrellas," I said, "this is the one I especially treasure."

She looked at it sadly, clasped her hands to her bosom and said, "Allow me." Taking off her pince-nez, she reeled in the chain until the glasses hung suspended from the capsule. There were two violet grooves in the skin of her nose where the glasses had sat. She bent over the box, and as tenderly as if it had been a child with a broken arm, she lifted the umbrella from the case and bedded it on the counter. She studied the handle and slowly unsheathed the sword.

"I know it is difficult," I said. "There are no longer artisans such as we have known, and for that matter there are no longer the umbrellas . . ."

"How well the Prince understands the time," she said sweetly. She breathed gently on the tattered Napoleon-blue silk. "I beg of you to leave it with me. I shall see to it personally." Putting a finger on her nose, she questioned and answered herself on the matter of the silk. Yes, she knew where to obtain the exact shade of silk that it had once been. "I shall restore it beautifully. I shall keep you informed of the progress of the work."

She took out a pad and wrote down my name and address.

She regarded me with a mixture of the profoundest respect and devotion, and made me the merest curtsy. "It is a great pleasure, *mon Prince*," she said. "A very great pleasure. The moment you entered this establishment, I knew, I knew at once."

I put on my gloves.

"There is," she said, "but I am certain you know of the incident in the history of umbrellas, but there is mention of an umbrella owned by Ludwig the Second, of Bavaria, who regarded as his royal prerogative the possession of the largest umbrella in all Bavaria. On one occasion he visited the Empress Elizabeth at Possenhofen wearing the uniform of a general and carrying in one hand his helmet and in the other his giant umbrella. The Empress happened to be standing at the window and broke into loud laughter, in which the King's entourage joined. His Majesty was furious. 'Why should I risk spoiling my hairdo,' he said. He was, as Your Highness must know, a great dandy, and wore white gloves to bed." She sighed. "Alas, everything is without romance, in our day," she said.

The little lady had called her workman who came bowing into the room. There was more instructive talk about umbrellas, their use in situations of danger.

In India, the lady informed us, an ordinary umbrella is the best protection against tigers. "One slowly opens and closes it, and the baffled beasts flee in fright. It scares snakes, bulls, and even elephants."

The workman was in truth beside himself at being assigned to repair the curio. With renewed assurances we were bowed into the street. There was martial music down the Rue de Rivoli, and the *Garde Republicaine* passed. It was the day the Queen of Holland visited Paris, and the populace waved Dutch flags and shouted.

The umbrella lady had put on her glasses again and her eyes shone through them with excitement. At the door, with the carcass of the umbrella still in her hand, she said: "Do not disturb yourself, *mon Prince*, the artisans we have them still. Yes, yes, they are still about and they are honored to do the right kind of work, for the right kind of client. We shall return this to

you like new; it will be better than new. I shall have a little gold
button put here to close it properly, with a blue elastic to match
the silk. You will have reason to be proud of it."

She curtsied again and disappeared into her shop.

"You win," I said to St. Cucuface.

"Half the streets are closed to traffic," he complained. "Everyone is made uncomfortable, and why? Because of the visit of
the Queen of Holland. Three plays are running in Paris now, all
of them dealing with kings and the past glory of France. In a few
weeks you will see the whole Place Vendôme blocked off and
decked out for the celebration of the birth or the death of
Napoleon, I forget which. And when you think of him, he gave
us nothing but misery; he ruined France and left her smaller
than he got her. Yet, if it were possible to bring him back, they'd
do it, and fall at his feet."

The umbrella was returned completely rehabilitated. It was
more beautiful than when he had first seen it, St. Cucuface told
me. Like all truly good things, it still was useful and appropriate. One could walk about with it in sunshine, carrying it folded
and attracting no attention, or open it in rain and be protected.
And one could draw the blade and defend oneself.

A FEW WEEKS LATER, the Aga Khan gave a cocktail party
and among the guests was the Maharajah of Bengal-
Something-or-other, a man of fifty, barely five feet high, who
carried himself with cock-sparrow stiffness. The jewels Bengal
wore were as big as the crystals of the chandelier. He stood at
the buffet with an equerry in attendance, and I heard him ask

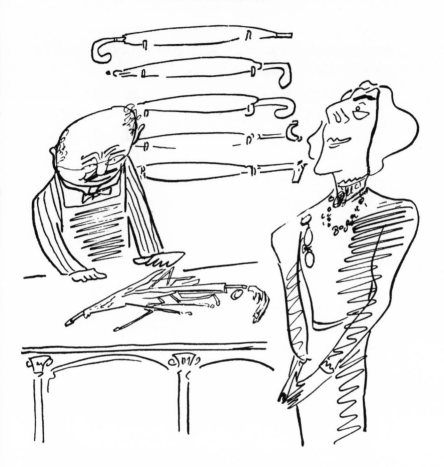

his attendant sharply: "What time does my spectacle begin?"
meaning, What time do we go to the theater?

The attendant said: "At nine, Your Highness."

"And now it is what?" asked the Maharajah, as if he were
biting ice.

"And now it is seven thirty-two, Your Highness," said the
equerry.

The Maharajah looked at a golden chronometer on his right wrist, and with a swift motion slapped back the sleeve from his left wrist and looked at another costly timepiece. He reached into his coat and brought forth a third instrument, a watch set with rubies and diamonds. He looked at this and said: "You are right, it is exactly seven thirty-two." He helped himself to some honeycakes and his equerry informed St. Cucuface that the Maharajah owned more than two thousand watches, and besides this collection, and matching it in value, he had the finest collection of umbrellas in the world.

"Excuse me a moment," said St. Cucuface. He returned with his umbrella.

The Maharajah took an immediate fancy to it, not even asking the price.

We saw Bengal a few days later, gaily parading along the Rue de Rivoli in his thin breeches and swinging his new umbrella, the Napoleon-blue silk matching the Maharanee's sarong.

At the end of the season the Maharajah and his entourage chartered a transatlantic plane bound for New York, where the Maharajah spent the winters.

The plane left Paris on schedule and stopped for refueling in Ireland.

The stewardess was busy in her pantry dishing up curry upon plastic plates when the even rhythm of the motors suddenly changed. A signal light flashed on, announcing: *"No Smoking. Fasten Your Seat Belts!"*

The stewardess left the pantry and went forward to the pilot's compartment. When she returned, her face was calm. With her reassuring, air-hostess smile, she went from chair to chair and repeated that all would be all right, if the passengers would remain calm. The plane had developed engine trouble, she explained. The pilot was returning to Ireland and hoped to make it without mishap. But there did exist the possibility of an emergency landing at sea.

A few minutes later there was another signal from the pilot and the hostess went forward again. She returned with the co-pilot and very efficiently they took from a wall locker a deflated yellow raft, capable of supporting the passengers, as well as the crew. When unrolled in the aisle, the raft reached the length of the cabin. It was the most modern, self-inflating type of raft obtainable.

The stewardess, who had been recently transferred from an overland route to the transatlantic service, had not yet become familiar with the lifesaving apparatus, and in her haste pulled the wrong cord, the one which caused the raft to inflate. In less than a minute, this instrument of safety had become a menace. At first it looked like a small yellow pig, then it was the size of a seal and a second later it grew into a whale. It began to move forward. The pilot was pinned against the controls, the co-pilot and the stewardess were gently lifted and pressed against the ceiling.

Puffing and hissing, the raft continued to inflate. The monstrous bag moved slowly toward the tail of the plane, in relentless pursuit of the passengers who had fled from their seats.

The Maharajah and the Maharanee kissed their children, embraced each other and bowed to the members of their staff. In the nightmare of these last moments there seemed no longer anything to do but to meet the end with dignity. The bodies of the distinguished passengers were now being mauled and flattened, without the slightest regard for protocol; arms, legs and

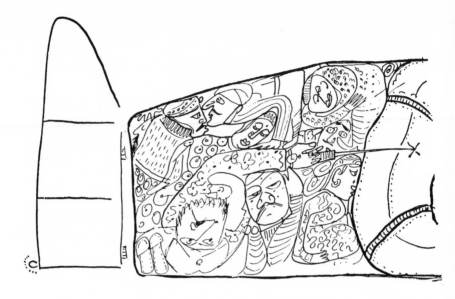

faces were pressed together like the truffles and meat in a *pâté maison*.

The raft had now become so swollen that it had moved up against the controls. It now flew the ship; it pushed buttons and, although it was still bright daylight outside, the signal lights began to flash on and off, bells rang, the landing gear was let down, and the drinking-water faucets were turned on. It had become very dim inside the plane, for the windows and the electric lights were becoming obscured by the swelling raft. The end seemed near. The helpless ball of doomed humanity was being rolled and squeezed toward the narrow tail of the plane. The unhappy Maharajah found himself standing on his head.

Fortunately, in addition to all his other interests, Bengal was also an ardent amateur photographer, and as such was ac- customed to seeing objects upside down and in dimness when peering beneath the black hood of his expensive camera. For in the position in which he now found himself, he saw his umbrella. Umbrellas are, as everybody knows, always taken by the stewardess as the passengers enter the plane, and hung in the wardrobe at the very end of the plane. With his last remaining strength, the Maharajah worked his right arm free, reached out and succeeded in grasping the St. Cucuface heirloom. He withdrew the blade and quickly thrust its point into the raft. The monstrous bag let out an agonized whistling sound, and then, with a long *hsss*, it gradually collapsed.

It was high time. The plane had begun a power dive when the pressure was relaxed.

The passengers slowly detached themselves from one another, the co-pilot and the stewardess came down from the ceiling, the pilot managed to regain control of both himself and the machine and brought his cargo to a safe landing in Shannon.

It was not long after this occurrence that a messenger from Cartier's delivered to St. Cucuface a solid gold and ruby cigarette case, from the grateful Maharajah.

"How mysterious is fate," said St. Cucuface, whose fate seemed to be to live by cigarette case. "One can readily conceive of such a chain of events being set off by the Prince of Bavaria—but never by a man called Bemelmans."

3.

Madame l'Ambassadrice

WE WERE SEATED in the Méditerranée, the restaurant that is home to me in Paris. St. Cucuface was eating *moules*, mussels cooked with garlic in a white wine sauce. He was eating them in the fashion of the French, that is, not with a fork, but with the shell of one mussel; using its sharp edge to dislodge the flesh of the others and then scooping up the sauce.

Three tables away from us sat a monk in most serious habit, his pale face framed in a short black beard. He also ate mussels and had a quart bottle of Muscadet, a light wine from the valley of the Loire, in a cooler at his side.

"He comes here once a month," said St. Cucuface. "He is a padre in an abbey in Normandy and, surprisingly enough, was formerly the director of the Casino in Deauville. He comes here as the guest of Jean Subrenat, who is the owner of this place." Monsieur Subrenat, who is six feet tall, sat down at the padre's table, and keeping an alert eye on the door for customers, said loudly enough for us to hear: "Oh, how fast time passes! This is a sad, sad day for me. Today at exactly five in the evening, the future father-in-law of my daughter will arrive here at the restaurant to ask me for her hand. Alas, all is arranged, and a good bottle awaits the agreement. An hour after that, at six, I lose my son also. He leaves for the Hotel Academy in Geneva, where he will, I hope, learn our trade properly. My son at least will come back; but my daughter has ideas of great grandeur in her head. She has chosen an architect. In these times! How she will miss her father's restaurant! She will think of it three times a day. She could have stayed here with me, and she would have had everything!"

The padre nodded. The mussels were finished. He wiped his beard and, turning his kind and intelligent face upon Monsieur Subrenat, he salted his worldly advice with ecclesiastic consolation. Then, picking up bread crumbs from the tablecloth with a moistened finger, he calmly awaited the next course.

Alphonse Girard entered and Jean, who considers all his guests his friends, told the famous painter the sad news about losing both his children. The children came in and stood about, the daughter a dark and beautiful girl as sad as the father. Saddest of all was the boy, who did not want to go to Switzerland at all, but must follow his father's orders.

Girard presented a seating problem. He was one of the most

esteemed guests of the Méditerranée, and one of the most distinguished painters of France, but he neglected himself badly. He never took a bath, seldom cut his hair, or washed his hands, and his clothing was as dirty and uncared-for as his person. The problem was solved by placing him at a window; the people on the other side of him were protected by a curtain of highly flavored fumes that rose from a copper saucepan in which small lobsters simmered over an alcohol lamp. It is one of the specialties of the Méditerranée called *Homard aux Aromats*.

"This is my luncheon," said St. Cucuface, as he called for the bill. The prices at this restaurant are fair, and a service charge of fifteen per cent is added. After St. Cucuface had paid, there remained three one-hundred-franc notes to put back into his thin wallet. He pulled out his ivory cigarette case and I was prepared to buy it again but he merely offered me a smoke. We had stepped out into the Place de l'Odéon when a waiter came running after us. He had a small package tied with a string. "For your little dog," said the waiter. St. Cucuface thanked him and took one of the one-hundred-franc notes from the wallet. "For my little dog," he said softly. "Some bones with a little meat on them."

I asked him whether there was a cocktail party that evening.

"Yes, there is. I have been asked to bring anyone I like. It's very small, but I think it will be interesting.

"Our hostess has her house on the Avenue du Bois. I am one of those Parisians who have never been able to bring themselves to call it the Avenue Foch. It's like the 'Avenue of the Americas' in New York which everyone still calls 'Sixth Avenue.'"

People of fashion eat very late in France, and cocktail parties often start as late as the dinner hour of the *bourgeoisie*. It was

seven when Cucuface pointed at a large iron gate on the Avenue
du Bois from which a wide pebbled road led to a château-style
town house. "This is her home," he said. "There is one thing
about her I cannot bear and which I feel I should warn you
about: she has a bad habit of scratching her head with a fork."

He rang the bell, the lock clicked and the iron gate swung
open. The wife of the concierge came out of the stone gatehouse
wiping her mouth with a napkin, and with her the stale vapors
of the close room and the mixed warm food smells of a finished
meal invaded the cool blossom-laden air of the May evening.

St. Cucuface inhaled the kitchen smell, complimented the
cooking, and guessed at what they had had for dinner. The little
woman's bulldog face broadened like a squeezed rubber ball.
She thanked him for the compliment and went shuffling back in
her felt pantoufles. "Very important, concierges in Paris, very
important to be friends with them," he said as we walked up to
the house.

On the first floor in a mirrored and tapestried room was a
maid dressed in a jacket like those worn by American motorcycle policemen. Behind her came our hostess uttering little
shrieks of pleasure. She had hair like Mary Pickford in the days
of silent pictures. The furniture about her was Louis XIV, all of
it with golden legs like toothpicks, and the upholstery was the
most raspberry shade of red to be found.

St. Cucuface bowed over her hand and introduced her to me
as Madame l'Ambassadrice. Although she had lived in France
for years, Madame l'Ambassadrice spoke with the pronunciation one learns out of small guide books. She locked St.
Cucuface in a mother's embrace. Her personality was as formi-

dable as her arms, and the room was so vast that I had not as yet become aware of the presence of two other people. After St. Cucuface had freed himself we saw them in the tall mirror over the buffet. They stood close together at the other end, so far away that the only thing definite about them was that they were men, and had thick black hair. St. Cucuface eyed them with suspicion as we were introduced, and he proved right, for both of them were Armenians about to poach on his preserves.

One was introduced as an artist; the other appeared to be his brother and the one with an eye for business. It was he who said: "Ah, Madame—let him meg a skatch of your divine fass." St. Cucuface's face darkened. Madame l'Ambassadrice put on a large garden hat and sat down and smiled. The other Armenian was instantly ready with a portable easel. He opened his gray shirt and from his hairy chest he took a leather etui that was suspended on a dark sweaty cord from his neck. In this he kept his pencils and brushes. The paper was already tacked to the board.

"It vill take only a miniut," said the other Armenian. The artist sketched very fast and made effective smudges on the drawing with his fingers. It was done in a few minutes.

"This iss only to shauw you vot ve can do," said the other as the artist held up the drawing. He had created something that looked like Greta Garbo at the age of seventeen.

Madame l'Ambassadrice lifted her lorgnette.

"Lovely, just lovely," she said. "Give them a glass of champagne, Cucu."

St. Cucuface looked at the picture in disgust.

"But it doesn't look like Madame l'Ambassadrice at all."

The artist's eyes flashed. "I paint the soul—not the likeness," he answered.

"That's right," said Madame l'Ambassadrice.

"How manny peepple you know look like beeing haalthy, and are maybe haalthy. And then they die—like zat—because inside is nothing no soul!"

"Yes yes—" said the brother, who was helping himself to champagne.

"On the other hand," continued the artist, "women who looks seek, finished, pale and broken, they always last forever. They never die." The artist motioned to the hostess.

"*Alors,*" said St. Cucuface. "You are not by any chance saying that Madame l'Ambassadrice is finished!"

"No, no!" screamed the painter. "Not at all. I am sayink that she is inside beautiful, and I have skatched the soul. Now I feel I must paint it, the soul."

"It needs color, Madame l'Ambassadrice," added the brother.

"I hope that you never paint my soul," said St. Cucuface.

"It vood look like a corkscrew coming out of a Swiss cheese," said the enraged artist.

"Boys, boys, boys," said Madame l'Ambassadrice and everybody got a glass of champagne.

"There is no time to loose. With stupid woman it hoppens soon," said the painter, trying to get back on his subject.

"What do you mean?" asked Cucuface.

"The inner life. You must paint it while it is still there; like a woman I vanted to paint. Last veek it was still there; she had it until day before yesterday, and now it's gone forever."

"Dear master," said St. Cucuface gallantly, "you must grant

that it is remarkable that Madame l'Ambassadrice, who is beautiful inside and outside, is also extremely clever." Madame l'Ambassadrice gave St. Cucuface one of her many grateful looks of that evening.

"Yes, with some women, it hoppens motch later. A peety that it hoppens at all," said the painter sadly.

The businessman-brother then drew Madame l'Ambassadrice into a corner where she listened to him with dazzled eyes. The painter stood guard over us.

"She has an incurable appetite for bums," said Cucuface. From long habit he was drawn to the buffet, beside which stood an ornate museum-piece of a table. On it reposed a silver humidor. Cucuface opened it and took six cigars from it. Seeing that I had observed him in the mirror, he generously gave three of them to me.

"Are you boys hungry?" said Madame l'Ambassadrice to the painter and his brother. She pronounced it, *"Avay-voo fame?"*

Before they could answer, St. Cucuface said sharply: "We have reserved a table for three at the Restaurant Lucullus, and it's getting rather late."

The two rugheaded Armenians had by now become openly hostile. After sending fiery glances in our direction, they departed without shaking hands with us.

Madame turned to the maid who had stationed herself with folded arms near the door.

"Monique," she said, *"voulay-vous portay* the tray with my dinner rings?"

A gray Rolls-Royce convertible of postwar design stood below and a chauffeur in uniform and cap to match beside it.

On the way to the restaurant, breaking a silence which had lasted from the Arc de Triomphe to the Alexander Bridge, Madame l'Ambassadrice remarked: *"J'ai un grande appetit."*

St. Cucuface leaned toward me and said, "Isn't it remarkable that a woman like Madame l'Ambassadrice, who has both great charm and great intelligence, should also speak the most beautiful French." She smiled a smile that lasted until we arrived at the restaurant.

In this exclusive and most carefully run restaurant, a reception committee consisting of doorman, door opener, coat hander, coat taker, inside-door opener, up-the-stairs pointer, director, headwaiter, assistant headwaiter and, further on, captain, waiter and bus boy, bowed and whispered: *"Mon Prince,* Madame l'Ambassadrice, Monsieur le Comte."

The director himself attached himself to the table to arrange the menu.

"Caviar—and the thinnest of *blinis,"* he recommended.

"Oui," said Madame l'Ambassadrice, with perfect pronunciation.

"A cup of *Germiny*—sorrel soup—with eggs beaten in it."

"Oui," said Madame and nodded assent.

"After, a little sole, with lobster claws."

"Ah, oui. I would like that very much," she said.

"Then a specialty of the house: a tender chicken of Bresse perhaps, in our fashion: sautéed, with *morilles,* which grow only in the month of May."

"Parfait—exactly what I want."

"A soufflé Armagnac—"

"Merveilleux, merveilleux," she sang.

"And to drink." The director closed his eyes, he sniffed at his

finger tips which he held cupped together close to his nose, as
though he were smelling a rose in bud. Then he whispered, "I
have something to offer you: a Rhine wine, 1920, made when
they pressed the grapes with the skin. There's only one bottle of
it left in the world. I have kept it for my best clients —*oui, alors* —
after that, Bollinger '34, Extra Dry." He stabbed the block on
which he had written the order with his pencil, signed his
elaborate initials, and thrust the paper at the second in command, who did an about-face and ran. The priceless bottle came
and was opened with every possible precaution; the inside of
the neck was carefully wiped, and then the director himself
poured the first half-glass. He rinsed it through his teeth,
washed it against the insides of his cheeks, and finally, tilting his
head back, he swallowed it, gurgling with delight. He seemed
unable to express his ecstasy in words and resorted to pantomime. Then, rolling his eyes upward, he poured the wine and
stood by to watch the effect.

Madame l'Ambassadrice said, "Chin-chin," and swallowed.
She looked at the director as he had looked at her, and repeating
his pantomime and rolling her eyes she said, *"Merveilleux."*

The director stiffened, bowed deeply and said slowly, "Always at your service, Madame l'Ambassadrice." He then
backed away bowing and it was as if Erich von Stroheim had
received the grand cross of the Legion of Honor.

St. Cucuface gave me a significant look. He had tasted the
wine and so had I. It was as dark as syrup and quite undrink-
able, something indeed rare and very difficult to obtain in even
a mediocre restaurant in France.

St. Cucuface tasted the wine once more, leaned toward me,
and shamelessly and while looking straight at her and holding

her hand tenderly above the table, he said: "Isn't it remarkable that a woman who is beautiful as well as intelligent not only knows how to order a magnificent dinner, but on top of that is a connoisseur of wines." Madame l'Ambassadrice looked at him meltingly. Then she picked up the caviar fork and scratched her head.

The dinner was very good and only spoiled by too much food and an overattentive staff. After the coffee and brandy, the waiter brought a small package tied with a ribbon. "For your dog, Monsieur le Comte, with our compliments," he said.

"They are so thoughtful," said Madame l'Ambassadrice.

We floated for a while in the bilious tedium of after-dinner conversation. Madame l'Ambassadrice said that she planned to fly to Cannes to meet the Ambassador, and that she intended to send the car separately with a chauffeur as she hated long drives. St. Cucuface looked very thoughtful and lit one of Madame l'Ambassadrice's cigars. He snapped his fingers and six waiters came running. Their faces dropped when Cucuface asked for the bill.

While the bill was being computed I wondered what would happen, for I knew that St. Cucuface had only two hundred francs in his pocket. They picked the one waiter who had an honest face to bring the bill to the table. It was upside down, lying on a gold plate large enough to hold a church collection. Then the company of bandits began to assemble. In a half circle about six feet away they moved restlessly about like sea gulls sailing hopefully over a ship about to dump its garbage. The lesser ones dusted tables with their napkins. All of them kept casting quick glances at the plate and all of them seemed near a state of inner collapse like gamblers seeing their last hope fade. They twisted their napkins in their hands, pushed chairs about, pulled at the lapels of their jackets, tailcoats, and on the ends of their noses.

None of them seemed able to leave the scene of impending disaster. There was the compulsion that brings a murderer to the grave of his victim. St. Cucuface studied the bill carefully and now they began to look at him with the utmost contempt. Some of them even gave vent to their feelings by slapping the napkins down on the cleared-off tables, pretending they were brushing away old toothpicks, bread crumbs and other dinner debris.

St. Cucuface then did an incredible thing: he asked for a pencil and began to add up the bill. Naturally he found several mistakes, none of them in favor of the guests.

Madame l'Ambassadrice was beginning to be annoyed. She

began powdering her face and looking at her teeth in the mirror of her compact.

"*Alors?*" she said, and managed to get an authentic French shading of annoyance into the word.

At this point there began a well-rehearsed pantomime of consternation, surprise and injury, played by the bandits. They stood in a row in back of the headwaiter, who impersonated an innocent citizen wrongly accused. He studied the bill carefully, and suddenly seemed to discover something. "*Ah, oui,*" he said, "we have forgotten something. We have forgotten to charge for the second helping of caviar that everyone had. As for the total, Monsieur le Comte, I am not Einstein, but I can add correctly. Where is the error? Show me." He set the gold plate down with a bang.

St. Cucuface took the bill. "Look," he said, and pointed to the error.

"Oh, that," said the headwaiter airily, "that is in the wrong column. *Alors,* that can happen now and then; it is merely an oversight of the cashier—"

"Let's get out of here," said Madame l'Ambassadrice loudly.

"Oversight! Why is it you never make an oversight in favor of the guest?" asked St. Cucuface.

The chorus now mumbled and made various gestures of hopelessness and disgust, such as holding both arms away from the body and shrugging the shoulders. They looked bitterly at St. Cucuface.

The restaurant was crowded, and Madame l'Ambassadrice had recognized several friends and had flashed friendly signals with her dinner rings at them.

"You are a band of thieves," said Cucuface loudly, waving his arms.

The headwaiter, on behalf of his staff, said: "*M-o-n-s-i-e-u-r.*" He said it very well and he stuck a finger in his high collar and pulled it forward for purposes of ventilation.

St. Cucuface and the headwaiter were now ready to begin the main assault. This fascinating contest is a necessary part of the repertory of every French establishment and reaches its finest form in a restaurant of the category called "*Exceptionelle.*" No one enjoys it more than the participants. The *aficionados* of this form of entertainment at nearby tables all turned their good ears our way. It promised to be a good fight.

Madame l'Ambassadrice spoiled it. She struck the table with her jewel-weighted hand.

"Shut up, all of you," she screamed.

The gallery nodded appreciatively. "Shut up," "Nuts," and "O.K.," and also "K.O." had been taken over into the French language. They approved highly of the "shut up" as being direct and expressive.

Unfortunately at this moment the director came to the table. He wore the widest of smiles, and completely spoiled the mood. He had in his hand a bottle of cognac so old that the label had been almost worn off by time alone. Fresh balloon glasses had been brought in, three men became very busy warming them in the palms of their moist and nervous hands, and then the golden brandy was poured with generosity and the compliments of the house.

Madame l'Ambassadrice said, "Chin-chin," and we clinked glasses.

"That is all very well and good," St. Cucuface started to say, but Madame l'Ambassadrice had had enough.

"You have nothing to say. This is my dinner," she announced imperiously, and produced a golden pencil set with rubies.

As if suddenly fresh candles had been placed on the tables, the faces of all the bandits lit up. The headwaiter paled several degrees from his former cockscomb red.

St. Cucuface tried again to engage him — but the mood was gone, the game was won.

The atmosphere of conflict had softened and the anger collapsed as softly as a child's balloon sinks to earth. Madame called the director and from behind her heavy iridium-and-sapphire make-up box, which she held to her face, she gestured with the emeralds on her right hand, waving green lights; a signal which everyone immediately understood to mean that she wanted the check.

St. Cucuface was not quite quick enough to take it as it appeared like magic. She initialed it and instructed the director to take ample care of the help in the matter of *pourboires*.

"I simply cannot understand you," said St. Cucuface. "Imagine — these robbers charging you four thousand francs for that Rhine wine, and then on top of it, making a mistake in adding up the bill. If you *will* put up with things like that — "

"I am sorry, Cucu," said Madame l'Ambassadrice. "I am very fond of you, but I will not have you making scenes in restaurants on account of your — whatever it is — outraged sense of proportion, or values, or something."

She put on lipstick and poked at her hair. She took the pencil and scratched her head with it. "It's the same thing every time we go out, Cucu, you and I, and I will not have it!" And then, remembering her perfect French, she added with finality, "*Je n'aime pas ça* at all! I forbid you to pay another bill."

"Well, if you want to be a fool," said St. Cucuface, "and if it makes you feel better, it's O.K. with me."

Madame passed the bowing heads and was handed down the stairs. The inner doorman opened the door of the restaurant and the outer doorman opened the door of the Rolls-Royce.

In the street, Madame l'Ambassadrice, whom we had permitted to drink the entire bottle of the rare Rhine wine, suddenly spoke English. The car was there, but not the chauffeur. She swayed a little and then she said: "Where is that old bastard?"

She informed us that her chauffeur made a habit of going into one of the *bistros* in the side streets while he was waiting and that sometimes he stayed too long and drank too much. We walked around awhile peering into various cafés, and the Restaurant Lucullus even sent out a posse of waiters to search in others, but nowhere was he to be found.

"The Prince is an excellent driver," said St. Cucuface. I took the wheel, and a few minutes later my incognito almost exploded: I drove the wrong way down a one-way street. A gendarme with the face of the true French flic blew his whistle violently. He crossed the street and approached the car with his notebook in hand. When he was close enough to see the license plate, he seemed to slowly arrive at the realization that this was an American car. He also began to remember the instructions of the *Commissariat du Tourisme:* to be polite to foreigners from hard-money countries. He gradually achieved a smile and touched his cap with a fat hand as he asked me for my license. I told him I didn't have it. "Your passport?" "I'm sorry, it's in my hotel."

He was joined by a colleague, to whom he gave the details. They held a long consultation in back of the car. Finally they came back and the first gendarme asked:

"You are a visitor here, Monsieur?"

"Yes," I said.

"Tell him you are an American," said Madame l'Ambassadrice, "and they'll let you go."

"You are American, Monsieur?"

"Yes."

"You have a very beautiful car," he said, smiling now like the full moon. "And if I may make an observation, you do not have the face of a 'gangster.'" They both laughed and swayed like musical-comedy cops. "And you say that your papers are at the hotel?"

"Yes."

"Well, we choose to believe you, Monsieur. Proceed. And Monsieur, if you insist on driving into one-way streets, sooner or later we shall have an accident!" He playfully wagged his finger and again saluted. We drove Madame l'Ambassadrice home without further incident.

Cucuface took the package for his dog out of the car and we waited until Madame l'Ambassadrice had gone upstairs, and then started home.

"In June it sometimes becomes very hot in Paris," he said as we walked back down the Avenue du Bois. "Also the tourists begin to appear in great hordes and take over the city. Then it is time to leave." I had to walk fast to keep in step with him.

"Do you object to long drives?" he asked. When I told him that I liked nothing better he said, "We shall do Madame l'Ambassadrice a great favor. We shall offer to drive her car to

Cannes. The chauffeur she has is quite unreliable, as we know; let her send him on a train. Of course she must pay for the gas."

After half an hour's walk, which ended along the Quai des Grands-Augustins on the left bank of the Seine not far from the restaurant where we had dined, we came to the house in which St. Cucuface lived. The building trembled every time the subway passed and since it was at the bottom of the incline toward the Place St. Michel, all the trucks and buses changed to second gear, and plaster rained softly down at night from the ceilings of houses along the Quai. We went up six flights of stairs, which sagged like those at the Hotel St. Julien le Pauvre, and became narrower as we came up to the *mansarde* of the building, in which the Count's apartment was situated.

I expected to hear the bark or the whine of a dog, but the place was silent as we entered, and a silvery light came through the large windows.

The view was sufficient compensation for the climb. Through a window, past a small terrace, one could see the Eiffel Tower to the left, and past Notre Dame to the right, up to Montmartre in the distance. And within this triangle was all that is most beautiful in Paris.

The moon was full, and the clouds were edged with the mauve and violet hues that Dufy smears into his pictures of the Paris sky. The beam of the searchlight atop the Eiffel Tower swept ceaselessly over the city, and overhead could be heard the soft murmur of the throttled-down motors of a transatlantic plane, its signal lights blinking on and off as it headed for Orly Field. Notre Dame was illuminated, and the light reflected from its white stones edged the towers and spires and the metalwork on the nearby roofs with a soft golden halo.

St. Cucuface opened the French window onto the terrace and came back with folding chairs. He pointed out various landmarks. "There is my Guardian Angel," he said, pointing to a golden figure on a roof across the river. He described the buildings and named the spires, and while he talked he slowly untied the package from the Restaurant Lucullus. He took from it a leg of chicken. He brought a folding card table, salt and pepper, a bottle of wine and a stick of bread which was neither long nor short, but of the in-between size which is called *un bâtard* in French bakeries.

Pointing at the lighted cathedral I asked if this was due to the observance of some special holy day.

"No, that we owe to the alert proprietor of the famous restaurant, the Tour d'Argent," explained St. Cucuface.

"A rich South American gave a dinner there for some friends on the eve of the Fourteenth of July—Bastille Day, our Independence Day—and on that occasion the cathedral was lighted, and from the windows of the restaurant which is on the roof the view of the cathedral is superb. One of the men who attended the party gave a dinner several days later, when there was no holiday. He was very disappointed that the cathedral was not lighted, and complained to the proprietor. To please his guests the proprietor then called the Secretary of the Diocese, and arrangements were made to light the cathedral. The price agreed on was then added to the bill at the restaurant, and now when you order dinner at the Tour d'Argent, the maître d'hôtel asks you what you want in the way of food and wine, and also whether or not you want the cathedral lighted. The money goes to the poor and everyone is happy. In such matters we French are exceedingly rational."

St. Cucuface poured wine and then went back through the window again. He reappeared with more dog-bone packages. "Let's see what we have," he said, and began to separate the various kinds of meat. Putting a bone to one side, he remarked, "Some of this actually goes to a dog."

He put the food away in the kitchenette of his apartment, which was tucked away under the various levels of the roof of the old house like a swallow's nest.

He then wrapped a bone in a piece of paper and tied it with the string. The Place Vendôme is an hour away. He offered to walk part of the way home with me.

Along the Quai des Grands-Augustins is a stone wall crowded with the famous wooden stalls from which secondhand books and old prints are sold. These were closed and secured with iron bands from which hung ancient and complicated padlocks. Along the stone wall is a break and a cobblestone roadway leads down to the paved banks of the Seine. On this part of the river, long, black barges are moored. They bear Dutch and Belgian names and are meticulously clean. Beyond a bridge, toward the Place de la Concorde, three gray fire-boats are tied up. Under the bridge a man and a woman slept back-to-back on a mattress, covered with a blanket and a tarpaulin bearing a stenciled U.S.A. Beside the mattress stood a baby carriage covered with a sack.

St. Cucuface made a chirping sound. The sack began to stir and out of the baby carriage jumped a small dog. As if he had never doubted his coming, or even known hunger, he stretched himself, yawned and waited politely until St. Cucuface had unwrapped the bone. He took it in his teeth with the utmost delicacy and made his way with great dignity to some stones

that lay in a patch of light that came from a window of one of the barges. In the light he showed himself to be a white, long-tailed fox terrier with a black mask. A few yards above, from beyond the bookstalls, the windows of the Restaurant Lucullus shone down. Occasionally there was the whistle of the doorman, the rattle of an answering taxi and then a sound of the doors being slammed.

The honking of the horns of the buses mingled with the rumble of heavy trucks laboring upward to the corner brightened by the glass-enclosed sidewalk terrace of the Brasserie la Perigourdine.

"Will you ever go back?" I asked.

"To the Restaurant Lucullus?"

"Yes."

"But certainly."

"Won't they resent it?"

"Not in the least. That was a comedy; I knew it and they knew it. I am one of the most scrupulous of people. There are those who would go back there and collect their percentage on the dinner, and they would get it without any argument whatsoever, and whenever they wished they could have a free meal."

In the pauses between street noises, the fox terrier could be heard crunching on his Lucullan bone, and the waters of the Seine murmured between the Quai and the barges and surged into two gurgling spirals, one at each side of the tillers.

"The trouble with me," said St. Cucuface, "is my appetite," and then, as if justifying something to himself, he added, "But you must agree that entertaining Madame l'Ambassadrice is difficult. I work like an acrobat. I saved her money by asking for the bill, for if she had asked, the amount would have been doubled. Also we are doing her a favor by driving her car to Cannes."

Two black-helmeted motorcycle policemen raced along the Quai.

"They can become rather nasty," said St. Cucuface when they had turned the corner. "Certainly so when you are a Frenchman. You were very fortunate that they didn't take you to the Commissariat and investigate whether it was true that you were an American. It could have been very unpleasant; they care nothing whatsoever for titles."

"But I *am* an American."

"Oh, yes, I had almost forgotten."

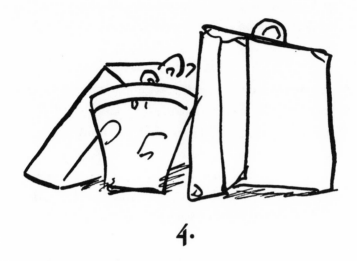

4.

The Perfect Marriage

DRIVING THE car of Madame l'Ambassadrice to Cannes, we stayed overnight at the Hôtel Carlton in Lyon and dined at the Restaurant Morateur, located in that hotel; all of it, including the city, depressing in a drumming, steady, ceaseless rain.

When we came the next day to Vienne, we wanted to stop at the famous Restaurant Pyramide, once, and perhaps still, one of the great temples of gastronomy. On that day the chef-proprietor of the establishment was in an off mood or else the publicity he had received had caused him to suffer from *folie de grandeur:* he had several near nervous breakdowns in our presence, screamed in his kitchen and behaved in his dining room like a police official, rather than a restaurateur. It is as damaging to a low *bistro* as to the best of restaurants, when the proprietor discovers that he is a rare and remarkable man with his pots and bottles. Upon seeing his picture in various publications and reading a description of himself he becomes obese with acquired personality.

The specialties of the house here, besides a fine dish consisting of the tails of crayfish au gratin, is the chicken from Bresse. I have followed pigs on stilts looking for truffles and I know a little about the growing of grapes and the bottling of wine and the making of brandy, but the raising of chickens of Bresse is still a remote subject to me. It must however be a mammoth industry in France; for while you get hams from half a dozen places and even the sardine cans bear the names of various regions, the chicken served in a good restaurant in France is always from Bresse, and it is an excellent bird, as everyone will agree.

I was able to arrest the attention of the proprietor of the Pyramide long enough to ask him about the chicken. He told me:

"Of chickens, I can tell you that they are never better than from September to February. Their meat then is well made and is not insipid. After February, the meat is not as tender nor as white. These we have now are young ones, four or five months old, and I am not too happy about them, for they have no character. We use them only for entrees. For the roasting chicken we must wait; it must be older; as for Bresse, I know as much about it as you do. I suppose Bresse to chicken is what Cologne is to water — some Eau de Cologne is made in Cologne, some in Paris. Some chickens come from Bresse; some people raise their own chickens of Bresse; some *Poulets de Bresse* are raised right here in Vienne. At least those I serve are."

The chicken we were served was cooked in cream, flavored with estragon, and it was so-so. The wine, not being subject to the temper of cooks nor the season of chickens, was of the very best.

Driving over the Route Nationale, Number 7, which is the equivalent of the old Boston Post Road in width and driving condition, we came to Toulon. We stopped there to have a tire fixed and St. Cucuface suggested that we make a detour and visit three castles, one called St. Cucuface and once his own property, and the others known respectively as the Château de Plaisir and Cucugnac, all located near Cucugnan, and Plaisir still owned by his aunt the Princess Eulalia Torricelli de St. Cucuface. We turned right on Route 527 (the roads in France are exemplarily and intelligently marked; your turn is announced long before you come upon it) and we came to Nîmes, a typical guidebook city. As we stopped to look at the arena, St. Cucuface sighed and observed: "Hereabouts lie some of the broken pieces of my childhood. It was here I always took my little cousin Ettore de St. Cucuface, and leaving him standing in the exact center of the arena, I would run for the exit, screaming that the bulls were coming." There are still bullfights in Nîmes, the kind at which no one gets hurt but the bullfighters, who prove their courage by plucking flowers from the horns of the enraged animals.

From here we drove to Cucugnan. One of the verities of travel is that the world is the same everywhere; the world of trees, of green fields, tilled soil and stone scenery and the

contours thereof. The road we were on might have been in
Bedford Village, New York; it resembled the stretch that leads
from the church there, out toward Danbury. At the left there
was the selfsame pale green water, the soft rolling hills. It might
have been also a road in Sussex, or the Austrian turnpike that
leads from Innsbruck to Salzburg. (The Rhone at times resem-
bles a bend in the Mississippi.) We came to a place of canals,
bridges, of Roman ruins, and fortified churches. The wide car
filled almost all of the road and we had to go into reverse to
negotiate a turn that brought us down a steep, cobbled incline
to a stone gatehouse.

At the gatehouse there was a sign, reading: *"Le château de St.
Cucuface—Admission 50 f."*

"I'll be damned if I pay admission to my own château," said
Cucuface as he got out of the car.

Outside the gatekeeper's lodge a small white goat lay under a
once-white metal table, and a black cat slept on the chair. On
the table was a blue paper block with printed tickets for admission to the castle. A third of them had been torn out. A man with
the dour face of the local peasantry appeared, supported by a
cane and shuffling in gray felt slippers.

He wore a cap, a muffler, a blue blouse and trousers that had
the stiffness of his legs and were bent in a curve, past the knees
down to his slippers. As he listened to St. Cucuface he lifted his
shoulders. Without any change of expression and barely moving his tired eyes and thin lips he said that he could make no
exceptions and that if the Comte de St. Cucuface, if such he
were, wished to visit the castle without paying, he would have
to take himself to Cucugnan, and there see the custodian of the

château and the person to petition. Unless he received the proper instruction—the doors would remain closed.

"This," said St. Cucuface bitterly, "is sufficient to wipe away all the nostalgia which has accumulated in my soul on the drive here."

He spoke again to the old man, who raised his arms along with his shoulders and stared at him with a mixture of contempt and suspicion.

"It will cost more in essence for the car than the whole thing is worth but it is a matter of principle to me," said St. Cucuface to me. "Do you mind very much if we drive the eight kilometers to Cucugnan, to see the Curé, my confessor, who will identify me? I want you to see my castle properly, not with a ticket in hand following a guide.

"In the person of that gatekeeper you have just met one of the sweet little people of France," he said as we got into the car. Along the road to Cucugnan, he delivered himself of some hard judgments.

"The good little people, those tender, gracious, all-understanding and charmingly immoral little people of France, every one of whom is a wine-sipping, cheese-nibbling connoisseur, a philosopher, and the custodian of our rural and national culture as well as a professor of the art of good living—ah, how I would love these little people of France, if only they existed. The ones I know are the most penurious race of men on the face of the earth. They live only in the imagination of writers of articles on travel, and in the melancholy, tear-and-time-dimmed memoirs of dreamers like Alphonse Daudet. They have carefully polished these spurious jewels until they glow like the gold and silver treasure of a cathedral. I must say that I have had more kindness from a cop in New York who once lent me five dollars when I had forgotten my wallet in the Long Island station of the Pennsylvania Railroad, than from any of them."

The Curé's housekeeper was hewn from the same wood as the gatekeeper at the château; she had his eyes and the lipless mouth, and she ushered us into the spotless waiting room of the rectory, a place of stiff white curtains, scrubbed floor and pieces of furniture that seemed to stand at mathematically appointed places. Not wishing to risk what remained of his nostalgia, St. Cucuface opened his wallet and took from it two one-hundred-franc notes which he put on a plate near the feet of a religious statue as the Curé entered the door.

The Curé de St. Cucugnan was slight, alert, quick in movement, and pleasant. He said that anything he could do to make our visit to the castle of St. Cucuface agreeable would be done. He offered wine and biscuits, and, having informed us that there was no restaurant worthy of our attention within fifty kilometers, asked us to dinner. He wrote a note to the gatekeeper of the château, and we returned there.

The guardian of the castle read the Curé's note. With unchanging unpleasantness he unlocked the high iron gate and swung it open. Passing under a private, small-sized arch of triumph we rolled down an avenue, the length of ten American city blocks and as wide as Main Street and lined on both sides with the black trunks of chestnut trees which had grown to their full height. There was the usual castle scenery of fountains, stone and ivy. What set it apart was that it looked comfortable, a place which would require only a small staff, not counting the gardeners.

"One consoling thing about this arrangement, in which the government has taken it over, is that they keep the place in perfect order," said St. Cucuface, pointing at the sharp-edged borders of flowers and grass, the trimmed trees, the raked and sanded walks and roads.

We had now come to the spot where one is always asked to leave the car to admire the view, the place where one says, "*Ah.*"

St. Cucuface left the car and with his birdlike stride led me to the vantage point.

Before us was a pond about a mile in diameter, the texture and color of pea soup, set in a molded, pale gray limestone frame. The neat practical château was perfectly reflected in this limpid, tinted pond. Two black swans floated exactly as they would have been placed by a photographer — one to the left, the other to the right of the castle.

This reflected scene of aristocratic self-sufficiency lay still long enough to take a picture, and then was disturbed by the bow waves of huge mossbacked carps that swam toward us. At the edge of the pond where we stood they halted and with greedy eyes and grunting sounds, like pigs trying to climb over each other into their feeding trough, they bobbed up and down and shouldered each other out of the way.

"They still remember my aunt, and my uncle, Count Hubert de St. Cucuface, who died without issue and left me this property. He was typical of his breed; even his valet used to say of him *vieille France* — he was truly 'old France.' If he lived today, he would be the president of the hunt and jockey club. His wife, on the other hand, would be president of the Society for the Prevention of Cruelty to Animals.

"In this difference of their natures lay the essence of their

tragedy. The marriage was arranged by both sets of parents; she came from one of the richest and oldest families; she was young and beautiful, and all would have been perfect, as such unions go, had they not unfortunately fallen deeply in love with each other.

"The evidences of their trials are all about you still. You will notice everywhere, side by side, there is the motif of the chase, and next to it, that of the Good Samaritan."

As we drove slowly around the pond there appeared among the greenery various pieces of statuary. From a distance they seemed deceptively alive, for all of them were of animals. As we drew closer half of them seemed to be concerned with hunting. Spaced between them were others, merciful and devout: Saint Francis talking to the birds, a lion at the feet of a hermit, doves drinking from a fountain.

"Looks like something the Russians might rent on Long

Island: a nice place in the country," said St. Cucuface. "No overpowering spectacle; no fountains, no needless terraces and Versailles staircases; comfort rather. You can ride around the property in an hour."

He pointed up a hill: "The Temple of Love," he said, "built in the first year of their marriage, before they discovered each other."

We stopped the car and walked up the hill through a rose garden. "You can always tell how things go with France by this garden. When we are at war, it is planted with potatoes, in times of peace it blooms with roses. Next year we may plant potatoes again. When I had it, it was all very untidy but somehow it seemed more beautiful than now. But then I am probably prejudiced.

"There is the brook in which my brother caught fish. Like most French boys, he was an excellent fisherman. The disgusting thing about that was that we had to eat them, to make him happy. The fish he caught had to be soaked for three days in vinegar, and still they stank of mud.

"Don't go into the temple now, it's damp, and you are still hot. Let's sit down and I will explain the landscape to you.

"That long low whitewashed house beyond the brook is the Old Men's Home. Just beyond it, you see, is the cemetery. An arrangement of great practicality, as such things always are in France."

Outside of the poorhouse, on a long bench, wearing blue almoners' suits and heavy boots, their hands folded over the crooks of canes, sat four old men. Their faces lifted like those of blind men, they leaned against the wall of the house, motionless as lizards, letting the sun warm them. The house was well placed, protected from the wind. St. Cucuface waved at the Curé who drove past below us. He sat next to the driver of a hearse; both men and horse were bowed before the wind and the black tassels of the funeral horse trappings danced.

"The *tramontane*," said St. Cucuface. "The wind from the mountains that makes one cold and miserable. The other, the warm one, is called the *mistral*. It tears at the nerves and makes one restless."

At the top of the hill, the wind tore at the black tassels of the horse's trappings, giving him the appearance of a great black crow trying to clear the ground. We went into the cool, dank Temple of Love.

Here again was the unexpected. Instead of the statue of the God of Love, which stands in all such edifices, there was a statue of Saint Sebastian. The figure was tied to a tree, and the body was pierced by arrows.

"My aunt had the figure of Eros removed and put this in its place. In their arguments, my uncle often referred to himself as Saint Sebastian being wounded by her arrows; also he was one of the few elected to that most serious sect, dedicated to hunting, the Society of the Archers of Saint Sebastian, who have their head-quarters in Bruges. He was the head of the French chapter and entertained its members here at the castle. This was their official statue. It stood in the dining hall; I'll show you where. . . ."

The hearse had halted at the Old Men's Home.

"What a curious world we live in, or rather float in," said St. Cucuface. "I say float, because no one, not anyone, has solid ground to stand on any more, not even in America. You would be surprised at the thoughts which burdened me as I looked across there at those old men a little while ago. My religion does not allow me to commit suicide, so if I live to be very old, if everything fails and I do not end up in a prison or a *maison de santé*, a 'house of health' as madhouses are called in France, I shall return here. As a combatant in the last two wars, I have preference on the Civil Service list and I might obtain for myself the position of concierge or perhaps even come to function as a guide in my own castle. Eventually, as I become senile, I will stagger over the hill to the Old Men's Home, and from there it is only a few steps into the cemetery. After a fashion, France always takes care of her own. Let us go."

The gatekeeper had arrived at the castle. He was picking out a key.

"That one of course is going to hold on as long as he can," observed the Count. "I'll have to wait until he vacates the post—it all goes by priority."

The old man opened the door and removed the cover from a postcard stand in the hall. We were in the usual castle hall of staircases, of doors to the left and right and between them six portrait busts on black marble columns.

"Again observe the hunting motif," said St. Cucuface as we entered the dining hall.

The scenes of carnage repeated themselves. A hunter rammed his mailed fist down the throat of a wolf. A dying bear sprawled with a lance in its heart and a wild boar lay on its back with a knife protruding from its side. Similar subjects, woven into tapestries, hung above chairs that were massive as choir stalls, decorated with angels and saintly figures.

The effect of the dining hall was that of a chapel except that at the end where the altar would normally have been there was an assortment of battle flags, two-handed swords, helmets and suits of armor. In contrast to this, at the opposite side of the room hung a life-size painting of a forest, a majestic stag with a shining cross between his antlers and Saint Hubert kneeling with folded hands before the animal.

Into the gilded frame was set a plaque on which was lettered *Thou shalt not kill.*

We walked up an ornate stairway to the private apartments. The bedroom of the Countess was in the tower, a paradise-blue room with a stucco ceiling of whipped-cream clouds. Here was pastel harmony. Panels of singing birds, of flowers and butterflies decorated doors and walls. The bath connected with a gallery that was lined with closets. The apartment of the Count was martial: cuirasses and crossed sabers and paintings of death in the field; even the porcelain of the washstand was decorated with fox-hunting scenes. The wastebasket at the side of his desk was the foot of an elephant; instead of a library there was a room given over to firearms.

There were the usual salons and reception rooms and a place where the Countess had sat near the window as long as she was well, and where sometimes, toward evening, she had played the harp. It looked exactly like the engravings one buys from the bookstall along the Seine. Her portrait, as sweet as the paradise-blue bedroom, hung in this room. From here we walked down and out of the castle. We crossed a pebble-covered yard and came to the north side of the house.

The wall at this side was built of blocks from the stone beds of Baux, the limestone that is crowded with the teeth, bones, skulls, scales and coprolites of fish, shells and reptiles; the furry air-roots of century-old ivy clung to its irregularities, and here the high walls of the chestnut trees met. I followed the Count through a mass of ferns and from this tiny forest we came out into the light into a brambly thicket, and pushing thistles aside walked a narrow path to a wide field in which hundreds of cattle lay about. Here stood a chapel, of the same stone and design as the castle. Beside it under a bent pine was a well, shaded by huge stones. Dead leaves, turned black, had sunk to the bottom and gave the water a leaden feel.

The white belly of a dead frog shone up in prismatic clarity, its limbs flung out as if it were stretching itself in sleep. We had disturbed the place. Masses of somber mothlike insects fluttered upward, and the silken snares of spider webs stuck to my face and hands. The place smelled like stale beer.

"Here is the exit of a secret passage from the castle," explained Cucuface, lighting a match and holding it aloft between two rocks. A little beyond us was the chapel. It stood in solitude, and birds flew in and out through an opening on the north end of the building. From a rosette window high above, colored by dusty amber glass, a shaft of light beamed down at the angle at which one leans an umbrella against the wall. The interior was dominated by two elaborate catafalques of black basalt. Into one was cut the name of Hubert de St. Cucuface; the other was plain and unoccupied. Atop the right one, with his head on a pillow of white marble, lay the statue of the Count, the debonair smile of his tribe about his mouth, his hands folded in prayer over his chest.

The body was hewn from hard, mustard-colored marble. The cut of the clothes was unusual: the figure wore a hunting costume and a hat; at his feet slept an alabaster dog, and beside him lay an arquebus.

"He prayed here for the fox and the wolf, and also that a miracle might bring about a change in his wife," said St. Cucuface. He pointed to the empty catafalque. "That was intended for her—but she is not buried here—and that is the mystery of St. Cucuface."

He picked some burrs from his trousers and tore a branch from a bush that grew inside the chapel, and with it brushed dust from the steps that were at the foot of the empty catafalque. He spread his topcoat for us to sit on, and widened his nostrils. "Smell," he said, "wild absinthe, rosemary and mint."

The beam of light had found the alabaster face of his ancestor and given it life: not that of blood and flesh, but the cold luminous existence of creatures that are deep in the ocean; the glow that is in astral bodies and specters conjured up at seances.

"When he first brought her here she was a child, and he not much more, he was twenty-five. And as I have said, they fell into the most abysmal kind of love; they could not stand to be out of one another's sight. They ate each with one hand holding onto the other's—and in the first years whenever he went to hunt, the farewell was tragic. For the length of time he was gone she fell into a state of deep melancholia. She was obsessed by a

82

Hindu-like worship of animals, and a dread of inflicting pain on anyone.

"Because he loved her madly and uncritically and granted her every wish he could read on her face, he denied himself the other great passion of his life, to which he was addicted as if to a drug. Only if you know the perfect harmony that is in the company of gun, horseman, horse and dog, can you appreciate his sacrifice.

"He put the horses to pasture, the pack of hunting dogs became house pets. They got fat and moved into the castle, where they slept in every corner of the place and lazily followed the Countess on her pigeon-and-carp-feeding walks.

"This was in the most beautiful period of castle life and in the golden age of hunting. Every year when the leaves turned brown, during the precious, short days of autumn when the first frosts set in, and the hunter suffers the pheasant fever — this was the worst time for my uncle.

"The quacking of ducks had supplanted the sound of the hunting horn, and as if they could read the calendar the pheasantry of the surrounding counties arrived in mass flights to take refuge in the forest of St. Cucuface. With them came the grouse and lapwings; I tell you, there were more feathers on the trees than leaves, and the low branches were scarred by the antlers of herds of deer. The wild boar was wild no longer; he dug his truffles undisturbed in the soft black earth, and the rabbits had their burrows in the vegetable garden.

"I suppose my dear aunt was the only one who deserved the 'Saint' in our name. To her husband she was a torturess.

"The happy husband and unhappy hunter became an object

of pity to his old friends as he wandered in the snow, over the lazily trotting tracks of foxes, for these knowing beasts had also adjusted themselves to the leisurely pace of the peaceful animal kingdom.

"The Society of the Archers of Saint Sebastian met elsewhere and the trusted, hard-handed servants and bumpkin stablemen were replaced by blank-faced cloister-voiced servants.

"The Count, whose every day had held a full measure of excitements and danger, and who had lived in leather and good hunting cloth, changed greatly in appearance. There is a portrait of them, painted at that period, she in a nunlike, pale-blue cowl, trailing a gown of mauve satin covered with a net of black lace, her favorite color, a pale blue look of kindness and love shining in her eyes. He sits before her, like the victim with his executioner; he is dressed as any one of twelve men in a jury box, his face is a zero—he had become like the pet mouse that she was said to feed from her tray every morning.

"It went on for years like that, in the isolation that love had inflicted on them, and he grew old in velvet jackets. For some time she swished through the halls in her collection of self-made pastel-colored habits and with an increasingly becoming pallor. And when she became an invalid, the devoted man who had given up his life to make her happy found his only joy in life in serving her.

"'I will do it,' he said when it was suggested that something needed attention. The household staff had strictest orders never to disturb the Countess. As time went on, the only service he allowed them as far as his wife was concerned was the bringing up of trays. He would descend the stairs and enter the dining hall and ring for the butler and say, 'Bring up the tray when the

Countess rings,' and then he would go out; fifteen minutes later the silver bell would ring, the butler would bring up the tray and there in her bed would be the old Countess. In a high, weak voice she would say: "Thank you, come back for my tray in ten minutes.' She would again ring the bell at luncheon time and the same routine would follow. Half an hour or so after the servant had taken the tray back, the Count would return from the forest and would immediately go up to see the Countess again.

"Now that she was confined to her room, a change took place in him. He seemed like his old self once more, his booming voice returned, on his walks he dressed in his hunting clothes and the evenings he spent oiling his guns. The old servants returned one by one, the dogs moved back to the kennels, the wild boars fled and the foxes ran. The old hunting friends returned and the annual dinners of the Society of the Archers of Saint Sebastian were resumed.

"The Count would enter the room on such occasions and greet his friends and then disappear, returning in a while to take his place at the head of the table. He would say that he had been with the Countess, and extend her greetings to them, and her excuses. He would then tell several anecdotes about her and would repeat conversations they had had. After meals he would disappear again and the guests would remark that surely in all the world there was no man so devoted to his wife as Hubert de St. Cucuface. The Countess had tea at five and dinner at eight. This life went on for years.

"One day, the Count left as usual for his morning walk, and when he did not return the servants went to look for him and found him dead, near the well, the place we just visited.

"After long deliberation it was decided that the butler, who was the oldest in service and the only one who saw the Countess several times a day, should be the one to tell her.

"He waited for the time that she usually rang but when an hour had passed and there was no sound of the bell, he went up and knocked at the door. He waited, and after a while entered. To his astonishment there was no one in the room. The bed was empty. He ran into the Count's salon and called the other servants. A thorough search of the castle was made but no trace of her was found. The Commissariat of the police was called, but first there came the guardians of the peace from Nîmes. These simple men were as puzzled as the servants. They were relieved by an Inspector of the Marseilles police and that one took the keys that had been found in the Count's pockets and he found that these fitted a closet in the tower, the one along the passage from his rooms to hers. In this closet were found the silken bed-jackets, robes, the wigs, and the night-gowns with which the Count had for years impersonated his wife. After leaving for his walk, he had made his daily re-entry into the castle by way of the passage from the well, to the stairway that led up into the tower."

A brace of ravens argued in a tree outside, and the bass voice of the herds of home-wandering cows sounded like a chorus of distant horns.

A bird flew into the chapel and seeing us, fluttered wildly above; his wingbeat disturbed the beam of golden light, and it splashed down on the alabaster face. For a moment, it seemed to become animated as if something had disturbed the sleeper. As we left, the caretaker accepted his fee with impatience and slammed the gate after us. In silence we drove to Cucugnan.

At the rectory the clean windows shone, the table was set, the plates and silver promised a good meal, and a bottle of wine was taking on the proper room temperature and from the kitchen came the smell of butter cooking.

The Curé read off the menu and then he began reminiscing about the Château de St. Cucuface. . . . "Years before the disaster I was asked to dinner there once a month, together with the veterinary—who was a protégé of the Countess. We both left hungry after each meal—for there was no meat or even fish at the table.

"At one of the last meals there, I made a *faux pas* during dinner conversation. Driven by hunger, I suppose, I said something about beef.

"I remember clearly the Count's face as he watched her, and her sweet voice as she said to me:

"'One never sees beef on the tables of India; that animal and its gentle mate, the cow, are too highly esteemed to allow anyone to murder them.'"

I have often wondered how old she was when she died and where the poor soul is buried.

5.

The Curé de St. Cucugnan

THE Curé de St. Cucugnan has an existence that might well be the envy of all sensible men. In the thin spire of his beautifully reconstructed church hangs a set of little bells that call the faithful to their pews. His secular duties pleasantly fill most of his days, and he has time to follow his hobbies. He hunts in autumn, he gardens in spring and he is a collector of old books at all times. His kitchen is of the sensible school of gastronomy, free of experiments and complications; the dishes of the region are varied and by repetition the best of them have been perfected. His budget remains balanced for although his income is small he receives constant gifts of food, of wine and even of cognac from his parishioners. His cook is wise and does not put his stomach to constant travail, inflicting punitive periods of digestion which, he informed us, make vapors rise to the brain, becloud the soul and fog the intellect.

The wine shone in clear glasses, and the main dish, a *pot-au-feu*—which, in the wrong hands, can be either greasy or watery, and a very dull dish, if not an ordeal—was here served in a porcelain tureen. It filled the room with its perfume of fresh parsley. St. Cucuface complimented the cook with a French proverb to the effect that she was one who knew how to make both rain and sunshine. When she had gone out of the room, the Curé said: "She also knows how to put a match to a powder barrel, but in the kitchen I give her carte blanche."

The Curé's face was gay, his gaze direct, he never pontificated, he told jokes and laughed freely; he was, as most French clerics are, good company and a free man.

The Curé wore his hair like a wig in the ancient fashion. It put him back a hundred years, the same period as a sermon he related to us, which had been published by the poets of Avignon, and concerned itself with the public of Cucugnan.

He told us that he found it ever beautiful, that even Daudet had copied it, that no one ever came to his house and left without hearing it, and that he exposed his congregation to it with excellent results once a year. "It's like an inoculation," he said. "It hurts a little, but the benefits are boundless."

We went into his study, and after giving us each a very bad cigar, he picked from his desk a small volume, worn and much thumbed. He sat down in a chair upholstered in leather once black, now rotted at the edges where white-capped upholstery nails held it to the wood. He lit his own cigar and gave us cognac of the quality of the cigars, quite undisturbed by the sounds of coughing and strangulation which came from our corner. His face was saintly as he looked over his glasses directly and sternly at us, waiting until we were quiet and listening, and then he began, as though he were reading to children.

THE ABBÉ MARTIN was Curé of Cucugnan. Honest as bread, worthy as gold, he loved all men and particularly his Cucugnanaise. For him, Cucugnan would have been Paradise on earth, if the Cucugnanaise would have but listened to him. But alas, the sinners shied from his confessional, and even on Easter Sunday only a few old women came to partake of Communion. The good father's heart was sad, for he was very old and ill, and he prayed daily to God asking to be spared long enough so that he might bring his lost sheep into the fold.

The good Lord heard him. One day the Abbé found the villagers assembled at a tavern and he rose and addressed them.

"My brothers," he said, "believe me or not as you choose; but the other night I thought the end had come. As you know I am very ill and I stopped breathing entirely. The doctor had given me up. To all appearances I was dead. Suddenly I, miserable sinner that I am, found myself at the very door of Paradise.

"I knocked, and Saint Peter opened the gate.

"'Oh, so it's you, my good Monsieur Martin,' he said. 'What good wind has carried you up here, and what is there that I can do for you?'

"'Good Saint Peter,' I said to him. 'You who are custodian of the great book and of the golden key, would you tell me, if I'm

not asking too much, how many Cucugnanaise you have in
Paradise?'

"'But certainly,' said Saint Peter. 'I have no reason to refuse
you this information, Monsieur Martin. Let us look together.'

"He put on his glasses and he opened the big book and turned
the leaves. 'Cucu'—he said, 'Cucu—Cucuface—Cucugnac—
Cucugnan—here we are; but you see, my good Monsieur Martin, the page is quite blank; there is not a soul here. Here are no
more Cucugnanaise than there are feathers on a pig.'

"'Is it possible?' I said. 'Nobody from Cucugnan here, not one soul? Please look again.'

"'Nobody,' he said sadly. 'Look for yourself if you think I am joking.'

"I clasped my hands, dear brothers, and I cried, *Misericordia!*' Saint Peter consoled me. He said:

"'Believe me, Monsieur Martin, there's no use of upsetting yourself. after all, it's not your fault if your Cucugnanaise insist upon doing their little stretch in Purgatory.'

"'Oh grant me this, dear Saint Peter,' I cried, 'Allow me at least to see them and to console them.'

"'By all means,' said the gracious saint, and taking off his sandals and handing them to me, he said, 'Here, put these on your tired feet, for the roads there are not too pleasant, particularly toward the end. Now go straight ahead, and after an hour or so you will come to a silver door and on it you will see a constellation of black crosses. Knock on that door and they will open it. *Adessias* and *au revoir!*'

"And so I walked and walked. What discomfort I suffered! I was goose flesh all over although it was hotter than midday in August. The path was lined with brambles, and further on it narrowed and was covered with glowing cinders. Near the silver doors, serpents sitting on glowing carbuncles hissed at me.

"'Who is knocking?' asked a rough voice.

"'The Curé Cucugnan.'

"'The curé of what?'

"'Of Cucugnan.'

"'Come in.'

"I entered and a beautiful angel with wings black as the night and a resplendent dress that was in contrast as bright as the light of day received me. The angel had a key of silver which hung from his belt. He was writing with a scratchy pen—*cra*—*cra*—*cra*—in a book that was larger than Saint Peter's.

"Without looking up the angel said: 'Why are you here and what is it you want?'

"'Dear Angel,' I said, 'I am curious to find out if there are any Cucugnanaise here?'

"'Who?' asked the angel.

"'Cucugnanaise—people from Cucugnan, for it is I who am their curé.'

"'Ah,' said the angel. 'You are then the good Abbé Martin.'

"'At your service,' I said.

"The angel moistened his finger so that he could more easily leaf through his big book.

"He mumbled—'Cucu, Cucuface—' He turned the pages and at last he came to Cucugnan. He looked up and he said, smiling: 'Monsieur le Curé, I am glad to inform you that there isn't a soul from Cucugnan in Purgatory.'

"'Dear Lord in Heaven,' I said. 'Nobody from Cucugnan in Purgatory. Good God, where can they be?'

"'Ah,' said the angel, 'they must all be in Paradise; where else can they be?' He began to give me directions. I interrupted him.

"'But I just came from there.'

"'Oh, you have?'

"'Yes, and they aren't there, not one of them.'

"'If they are not there and they are not here, then there is only one other place where you can find them,' the angel said sadly.

"I broke out in tears and I said to the beautiful angel, 'How will I ever get into Paradise myself, and if I should get in, how could it be Paradise for me if my beloved Cucugnanaise weren't there?'

"'My poor Monsieur. Since at whatever cost you wish to assure yourself of the whereabouts of your Cucugnanaise—here, take this pass, and if you know how to run, then run. You will find a portal to the left and there they will give you the information you seek. *Adessias!*'

"I found myself outside of Purgatory; the silver door had closed behind me.

"Oh, it was the hottest road I have ever been on, being, as it was, paved with live coals. At every step I swayed like a reed from faintness. I stumbled, I faltered, I was soaking wet and on every hair of my body hung a great drop of sweat. But thanks to the sandals which the good Saint Peter had lent me, I was able to proceed without burning the soles of my feet.

"Reeling along this road, I suddenly saw to my left a gaping portal like an immense oven door. Here no one asked my name. Great crowds of people went past me in masses. They entered the inferno, my friends, exactly the way you go to the cabaret on Saturday night.

"I was sweating more than ever now, and at the same time I was chilled. My hair stood on end as I smelled the stench of roasting flesh and burning bones, a smell something like the one here in Cucugnan when Eloy, the blacksmith, shoes a donkey.

"'Hey, you—are you coming in or not?' croaked a horned demon, prodding me with his pitchfork.

"'I—I'm certainly not coming in,' I said. 'I am a friend of God.'

"'If you are a friend of God, you old pious bastard, then what in hell are you doing here?'

94

"I could hardly stand on my two legs.

"'I have come a long and tortuous way, to find out if by any chance you could tell me if you have anyone here who is from Cucugnan.'

"'Are you trying to be funny? As if you didn't know that the whole of the village is here! Take a look.'

"I looked. In the very center of an overwhelming burst of flames was Galine. You all knew him, my friends. You all knew him, the one who was always drunk and beat his poor wife.

"I saw Cathy, the little whore who always had her nose in the air.

"I saw Pascal of the sly fingers, with which he pressed oil for himself from the olives of Monsieur Julien.

"I saw Babette, the reaper, who seduced the husband of her best friend.

"Oh, I saw them all — Dauphine who sold the water from his well during droughts, and Tortillard who passed through the church without ever removing his cap or taking the pipe from his mouth. All of them were there.

"My eyes smarting, and pale with fear, I took a last look and recognized a father here, a mother there, a grandfather, and brothers and sisters of you — far too many to mention by name.

"You well understand, I hope, how I felt after I had seen all of this. So when the good Lord allowed me to open my eyes once more, I immediately made up my mind that these things could not go on.

"I am in charge of your souls, and I have every intention of saving you from the abyss toward which you are rushing headlong.

"Not later than tomorrow I shall set to work, and I shall

certainly have enough to do. This is the way I shall do it; for in order that all be well, I must proceed in an orderly fashion. We shall take it step by step.

"Tomorrow, which is Monday, I will confess the old men and the old women—that should be relatively easy.

"Tuesday, the very little children. That won't be hard either.

"Wednesday, the boys and girls—that will take time and patience.

"Thursday, the men. That will run into the late hours.

"Friday, the women. I shall have to tell them to be brief.

"Saturday I have reserved for Monsieur de St. Cucugnac. That is not too much: a day for him alone.

"And if on Sunday we are finished, then we can indeed be proud and happy.

"So you see, my dear children, when the wheat is ripe it must be cut; when the wine is drawn it must be drunk; and when the linen is dirty, it must be washed, and washed well.

"God bless you, and Amen."

THE CURÉ DE ST. CUCUGNAN closed the small book.

"Thank you for a beautiful story," said St. Cucuface.

"It is very effective still," said the Curé. And it was, for we had intended to leave after lunch. It was Saturday. Suddenly St. Cucuface found some ruins to inspect, and also a local museum, and during the afternoon he directed his steps toward the church and went to confession, and we stayed overnight so that he could attend Mass and Communion the next day.

The church was filled, and the singing was accompanied impressively by an electric organ of American make.

6.

The Château de Plaisir

THE CURÉ invited us to a late breakfast after church, but
Cucuface, although he had fasted that morning, said that we
must drive on to the Château de Plaisir, since we were expected
there for luncheon.

We drove on a winding road past rocky fields of pine trees
and cypresses, and into a forest where the car wobbled over the
roots of century-old beeches. The forest held the morning fog
and the gray trunks of the trees near us seemed outlined with a
sharp pencil line and set apart against the gray wall into which
both trees and fog melted in the distance.

The ground was covered with the light brown paper-like dead leaves of the beeches, and the new, trembling pale green foliage closed overhead.

It was hard to see the road ahead. I turned on the headlights, and the dragging mists lit up and completely obscured the road. I turned the lights off again and we proceeded, with St. Cucuface walking ahead as a guide. The hood of the car was covered with steaming moisture and Cucuface announced that he was getting hungry.

We drove on over stones and roots, and in a long hour we emerged from the forest and came out into clear air and upon a scene of great beauty. Set into a sea of grass, smooth as green linoleum, newly mopped, the Château de Plaisir rose from a hillock, in the exact center of the landscape. The approach was through an aisle of poplars, planted at exact distances from each other to the left and right, each one at least fifty feet high.

The castle itself was as black as if it had been built of coal. Small clouds sailed across the sky and passed before the sun, the change of light effecting various shades of gray and black. Occasionally a roof flashed in silvery light. The massive towers had strong shadows on their flanks and the dark symmetry of the façade was forbidding, for there was nowhere any relief from the cold solidity of its design and I began to suspect that one could be quite cold and uncomfortable inside.

Spun out over the landscape, the longest way around, against the border of forests that surrounded the castle on all sides, was a white wall, on which the eye could exercise itself interminably. It followed the smooth contours of the land, up and down, remaining always visible. The two ends of the wall came together in front of us; we were now driving toward the last of the poplars. There, ornamented by two stone towers, and guarded by black gargoyles from whose yawning mouths rainwater dripped, was the gate, on one of whose bars hung a flower-framed sign saying "Welcome." When we sounded the horn, there was an answering metallic click, and both halves of the high gate swung back automatically, and automatically closed behind us. "American," said St. Cucuface. From the gate it was a distance of about three hundred yards to the castle, driving on an avenue of pale yellow sand which cut through the green linoleum, with all the colors freshened by the rain. The property was in perfect condition. My friend put his hand on my arm.

"I should explain that Aunt Eulalia is a little odd. And by the way, if you happen to know—and you probably do—the Duke of Milfuegos who now lives in New York, please under no circumstances mention his name."

As we rolled on, a model dairy with an American-type silo appeared and, their shining hides matching the wet black Château de Plaisir, a dozen Black Angus cattle came into view.

"She knows every one of the principal distractions of this life. When I last saw her, she had alabaster skin, her hair was carrot red and her eyes were like lapis lazuli. Being part Italian, she has the appearance but not the talent of a great diva. She was esteemed, be-sung and feted, and Berlioz is said to have dedicated a triumphal fugue to her. I suppose she will have a mustache by now, but she will still drink us both under the table. She is a ruthless *aficionado* of Life. Here we go; turn left, go up and in through the second gate."

The car rose to a court of honor, dominated by a massive oak. The gloomy mood of tone and age that cloaked the outside of the Château de Plaisir changed here to warmth. Again the scene was unusual and one that the eye of the onlooker could absorb instantly. From the center of the court rose an oak so old that it would have taken four men to embrace it. The branches of the tree had twisted themselves upward between the four walls and covered all the free space, the leaves so close together that they looked like thousands of green gloves hung up to dry. The walls were a pale yellow and the pavement of worn brick slabs, each the size of a bath mat. The brick had almost absorbed the water; the center of each slab was dry. It all seemed scrubbed and institutional; nuns or nurses belonged in the courtyard. A carillon began to play: *Klink, klonk klunk — Klinkityklunk klank klunck klinck ∂i klanck.*

A peasant woman in a wide blue skirt with a pan on a stool before her cleaned some vegetables. She looked up and smiled at us.

"Exactly as it was always," said St. Cucuface.

Suddenly through the *klink klonk klunk* the voice of the aunt blasted. The echoes of the bells banged back and forth between the walls and St. Cucuface ran to be received. The old Princess's skin was alabaster still, her deep blue eyes shone, and she smiled and pressed her mustache on the face of her nephew — it was as if he had put his face into a soft white pillow. A pack of dogs had come down the stairs: fox terriers mainly, with their offspring, none of them with ears or tails clipped. They at once began to inspect our trouser legs. The Princess, in a purple, tasseled robe, such as a cardinal might wear at Easter, pushed the sleeves back from her wrists, turned and, with arms waving, began to make her way back into the château.

The interior had the mood of the Salzburg Festival sets for

Rosenkavalier. The first was a comic grand-opera living room—a huge gold-colored cape hung near the door under a hat with a large green plume. All of the furniture was oversize, even to the footstools, which would have made a bed for a great Dane. From the vast stairway hung Spanish shawls and battle flags, both embroidered in the loudest reds, greens, and yellows. A brass lamp of many colors and the size of a laundry tub was suspended on a red silken hawser. Under a painting of the Princess, showing her in mauve veils and an Isadora Duncan pose, stood a black Bechstein concert grand piano. It was closed, in order to support a vast collection of photographs in various sizes and important frames and each bearing the determined penstrokes of important people. In addition were sofas for giants to rest on, deep easy chairs, bushes of white lilacs and azaleas in large red vases, albums of opera music, busts of composers, copies of various musical publications, opened letters, and small silver dishes everywhere holding sweetmeats, candied citron, lemon balls and other fruit candies.

The Princess moved about in all this, floating here and there like the clouds over the castle, her arms rotating about her. She was immense but without weight, she had the quality of baked goods, of soufflés, babkas, and brioches, she was fateful, important, motherly, but not sad.

"Prince de Bavière, is this not a little like Bavaria, like Munich? Is this not like Nymphenburg?" she had asked me as I had been introduced to her in the courtyard. She swept her arm over the scenery and out to the white wall.

"*Ach, Gott,*" she said. "Vienna, Bayreuth, and Munich—and Rome. And now I hear Lauritz Melchior is singing in a cinema." She offered a dish of candied grapefruit peels and looked at the floor, a worried, searching expression on her face. It passed the moment she saw what she was looking for. "Come here, Caroline," she said, and pointed to a turtle the size of a dinner plate that lifted itself on its scaly legs.

"The darling," she said. "The dear creature. I must explain. I cannot make a fire here all winter, because Caroline—" she paused and used a pet name of Viennese origin: "*Das Viecherl da*" which means "the little animal there"—"because *das liebe Viecherl* takes her winter sleep under the logs in the fireplace. She hibernates there, and curiously enough, she came out today; she always comes out when I play. It is a remarkable thing: I have a radio and phonograph of American make, and she does not come out for the news, or the BBC, or for symphony or tangos; but when I play the piano the darling appears. This morning I played Schumann, and suddenly I heard a rustle, and there, *das liebe Viecherl* slowly came out of the fireplace, blinking, to say hello to me.

"Here, Caroline, darling." She took a small frosted sugar wafer, and Caroline lifted herself again and opened her horny mouth. She took the sweet and dragged it under the huge sofa.

"Now we must go and eat, or else my chef, who is very temperamental, will stab himself with his big knife.

"You will be surprised, Prince, and you will be doubly surprised, Cucu: we are having a completely American luncheon today. I had a visitor from America who brought me gifts."

She looked very sad as she said that and folded her hands very tightly, as stammerers do when they are unable to speak. She went to her various supply depots and picked sweetmeats from the silver dishes.

"Allow me to read the menu," she said as we sat down.

"Alligator pear with grapefruit, an omelette with capers, terrapin à la Maryland . . . I feared that this by itself would be a little soupy, so the chef and I decided to have some truffles baked in pastry with it. A specialty, Prince. Truffles cooked under hot cinders, he does them very well. After that, we're having some cold Virginia ham and cold goose with aspic, a little field salad and for the dessert, a *bavaroise,* made from fresh pineapples. Simple but good," she said and suddenly, in a voice like the anguished cry of the Valkyries, and of a volume sufficient to summon the countryside if her house were on fire, she called for the butler.

"He doesn't hear very well," she explained.

He came and opened the first of five bottles of wine in a

massive cooler which stood at her side. "He is as old as the *Viecherl*," she said as he poured the wine. "If only he were as intelligent."

"When were you born?" she asked me and then took my hand and looked into it.

"Look, Cucu, what a future he has!"

"Have you ever been to America?" she asked. "I have never been there."

"I would like very much to go to America again," said St. Cucuface.

"For a visit?"

"I'd love to go there to stay, to settle down, to work."

"To work at what?" asked the Princess, putting away the spoon with which she had been eating the alligator pear.

"To be a chauffeur," said Cucuface. "I want to start at the bottom and remain there."

The Princess stared at him.

"He never changes," she said. "He talks always nonsense."

"I have never been more serious," said Cucuface. "It is the only free profession left, that of chauffeur; besides I love fine cars."

"You mean a chauffeur of a taxicab kind of car, like the Russian grand dukes used to do in Paris?"

"No, no, a real chauffeur with a uniform."

"What a curious idea," said the Princess, and turning to the butler, who was also out of grand opera and had been born to stand with a silver candelabra in his hand, she screamed, "We're ready for the omelette."

"*Er hört gar nichts — mehr*," she said to me.

"Go on, Cucu —"

"If everything fails, I shall go to America and be a chauffeur for a rich Negro," said St. Cucuface.

"What?"

"They are extremely interesting, gentle and understanding people, and the best of employers. I would be treated as a friend. I would never be made to feel my position. Besides, in America the Negroes own all the beautiful, white-tired, immense new cars."

"How very interesting," said the Princess, without conviction. "I didn't know about that. Tell me more."

"I live by design, my dear aunt—imagine the elegance of it. A great, black, stupendous Cadillac, with white upholstery and white-wall tires outside; a chauffeur who is a count, with a white face in a black uniform in front. In back a black man with a white tie, in a black hat, the whites of his eyes shining, a cigar with a white ash in his black hand. Suddenly the black man will slap his leg with his white gloved hand and break out in loud laughter, the fine rich laughter of which only the Negroes are still capable. . . .

"And he'll say something, I don't know what, I only know it will be like poetry and that it will make me happy."

"But you are mad—At any rate, I suppose, it's more honest than marrying a rich American girl for her money." Lifting her glass, the Princess let out a new fanfare, calling the butler.

"*Klunk—Klank—Klingkinkling*," went the carillon.

"I never can say no to a *fiesta*," the Princess announced as she peeled a crust of pastry from a smoking truffle the size of a billiard ball. "Oh, the parties we have had, the dances, the music and the laughter—*die herrlichen Zeiten*—that will never come again. Apropos of that—we are all invited to a costume party tonight, at the Château de Cucugnac. The new owner, a Monsieur Rosay, from Lyon, is giving a ball."

"But we have no costumes," said Cucuface.

"It is all provided for. We dress; for those who don't have costumes, the provident host has made arrangements."

She took hold of the tails of the butler's coat and pulling them as one pulls a bell cord yelled at him to open another bottle.

"*Ach die liebe,*" she said and looked at the floor. The turtle was approaching the table.

"The painter Dali once told me that turtles are very useful. They make excellent ashtrays," said St. Cucuface. "The way to do it is simple: you take a turtle of medium size, a young one,

preferably between fifty and seventy-five years of age, and you have a jeweler attach a metal rod to its shell. On top of that an ashtray is put, a detachable ashtray that you may take off in order to have it cleaned. The advantage is that since the turtle always tries to get under something, it will always be next to a couch or an easy chair where you want the ashtray."

"Very practical," said the Princess.

"And besides," added St. Cucuface, "when you leave, you can say to the housekeeper—'Good-by, and don't forget to feed the ashtray.'"

The dessert was served and the Princess signaled the butler to bring the coffee to the music room. There the retinue of small dogs appeared again and they sat about her on the large sofa, each one in his appointed place. She fed them sweets and then poured coffee. She smoked a Cuban cigarette in dark paper with a golden mouthpiece, very slowly, like a beginner. For a while, she leaned back and talked of her memories of the musical world of Vienna, Munich and Rome.

She suddenly called the butler, who had become expert in getting her out of her deep chair. Employing an elaborate system of grips, he had the Princess standing up in three moves. She then proceeded to leave the room under her own power, preceded by the fox terriers. The cardinal's gown seen from the back was a swaying tent with a large tassel and a decorative triangle of needlework, varicolored as a cathedral window, set in between the shoulders. As she progressed toward the stairs, the tassel was affected by the majestic rhythm of her walk: it swung slowly like the pendulum of a great clock.

"It's almost four. It's quite late now," said the Princess without turning around. "Get some rest; and don't forget—there's a party tonight."

The butler brought a dust-crusted bottle of brandy and a box of cigars. There was a scraping sound as the turtle moved somewhere in the room.

"I am cold," said St. Cucuface. "I'll ask him to light the fire before *das* darling *Viecherl* there decides to resume her hibernation."

7·

The Postponed Wedding

THE COUCH was soft as a mudbath. The postprandial fumes, of which the Curé had spoken, ascended to the brain and obscured the mind. I wakened after a while and heard a mellow snore from the other end of the immense sofa where St. Cucuface lay buried.

I looked at the painting of Eulalia Torricelli de St. Cucuface on the wall above me. She had been a great beauty then, a model that a painter might have sought all of his life. And placing beside it the Princess as she now was, one saw that while the pulse had slowed and beauty was gone, pride and personality had remained. She had become grandiose. It was the meta-morphosis of the young grape to the rare brandy in a well-cared-for bottle.

The bells rang again: *Klink klank klunk. Klank klank kliing* — sounding far off. The *Viecherl* seemed to have decided to eat the sugar wafer at last, for a tiny sound of crunching came from beneath the sofa.

St. Cucuface awakened.

"If you can get up," he said, "go over to the piano and collect the *personae* for the drama of the Château de Plaisir. They're all there, all but one, Mr. Bullwinkle, whom I shall describe to you. But first, bring the picture of the man who is both the hero and the villain of the piece. You'll find him to the right among the largest frames, somewhere among Alfonso of Spain, Umberto of Italy, and the last Pope before this one. He's in a silver frame with rose jade corners; the one you have your hand on now — the Duke de Milfuegos."

The face of the Duke was divided as in a Rouault painting. Centerpiece: a parsnip nose long and flat down the middle; a horizontal centerpiece of black: a mustache. The rest: narrow forehead, black hair, and a thin chin, also elongated. Dark sad eyes, dark skin, and a circular depression the size of a penny under the broad-lipped mouth.

He leaned forward in the photograph, in the tight uniform collar with decorations at the neck, on both sides of the chest and also at the hip. One gloved hand rested near the diamond-studded star at the hip and the other on the hilt of a sword. The signature was like a whiplash.

"Now go down to the left; pass over Caruso, Pavlova, Emmy Destinn, Farrar, and past that fat man there who was the great opera singer Slezak; you come to a picture of a sad and soulful young girl in a gold and ivory frame; that is the heroine and the rival." I picked up the picture. On it was a young woman with large dark eyes, a pale round face, sensuous mouth and hair combed tightly back under the brim of a sailor hat. "That is Consuelo."

"It's a very small cast."

"You may not know Mr. Bullwinkle, but I am sure you have seen him a hundred times in New York. He's an egg-shaped man, with a face the color of liverwurst that has been overexposed to the air; he wears thin mustaches which look as if he were carrying two little dead mice in his mouth, whose tails hang out at the side.

"He accentuates his odd appearance by his dress, and wears suits that are of the period of Napoleon the Third: narrow trousers, and a *pet-en-l'air* kind of covert-cloth coat, with old-fashioned collars that were called '*Vatermörder*' in my childhood. Add to this a Churchill hat, yellow gloves and a thick bamboo cane. His appearance is such that once a well-known comedian, whose stock in trade is painted-on eyeglasses, a short cane and a cheap fur overcoat, stopped him on the street one day and said: 'It's people like you that spoil my business—you do it for free.'

"Now be so kind as to put them back. My dear aunt would have a heart attack, if she should appear unexpectedly and see us rummaging in her past." He settled himself deeper into the sofa.

"I find all plots dull, so I shall run through this one as quickly as possible and tell you what you must know in order to understand what follows:

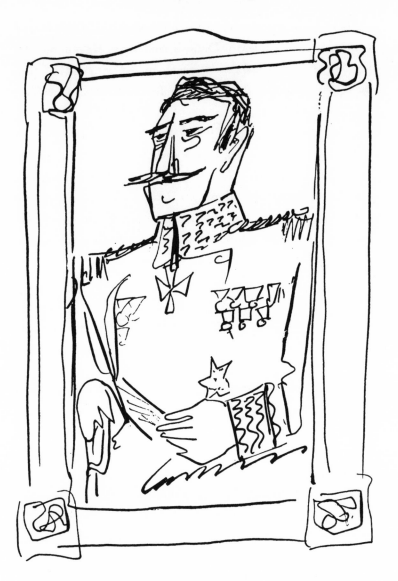

"In the province of Catalan, on his mortgaged castle near the town of Figueras, lives the Duke de Milfuegos. He is approaching the end of his youth, and is deeply in love with and in return deeply loved by Eulalia, Princesse Torricelli de St. Cucuface.

"First Act—

"The Duke comes riding across the border. He asks for her hand and is accepted, *Tara tara tara—boom boom.* There are visits back and forth, there are letters every day, flowers, dedicated bulls, smiling relations, courtship on horseback, tears of happiness, announcement of marriage, celebrations, and guests in the house. Intimate concerts at which Eulalia sings to his accompaniment—heavenly bliss and Curtain with a bang.

"Because the Second Act opens with half the cast in black. The mother of the Duke has died of old age, flowers again, black borders on the stationery, the marriage is postponed, and just as this period of mourning comes to an end, the father of the bride is killed in a hunting accident in the forest of St. Cucuface. Again tears, the deepest mourning; the church bells tolling slowly are the only music now—and the date of the marriage is again changed.

"The Third Act is as tearful as the Second: four years have passed since they first met. The beauty of half-French-half-Italian girls fades quickly, but even more damaging to happiness is circumstance. An accounting of the estate of Eulalia tends to age her even more. The unhappy Duke begs to be allowed to withdraw. He writes the most beautiful of farewell letters and vanishes, seeking his fortune across the sea.

"Too proud to seek the pockets of relatives, Eulalia tries to

make a career. She lives frugally in Rome, Milan and Vienna, she is beloved by everyone in musical circles, but her talent does not justify a career. Now, with her young beauty faded altogether, but at the beginning of the stage where the Italian and French women take on a second bloom, the beauty of a fortress which improves with age, Eulalia returns. She is a resolute woman. At first, she tries to sell the castle, but it is too shabby and isolated to find a buyer readily, and at a good price. Next she busies herself making the immediately necessary repairs. She buys a dozen little white beds and washbowls, and turns her castle into a boarding school for young girls of good family. She advertises the charm and isolation of the Château de Plaisir in the most conservative journals of France. Surely, the great name of the place and owner will crowd the place. The problem will simply be whom to refuse and whom to accept. But again poor Eulalia fails, for France is studded with boarding schools for young girls and some people prefer to send their children to the thousands of boarding schools in Switzerland.

"At long last she receives a letter of application from the parents of a little girl, an 'unusual' child, as she was designated during the early correspondence. The child turned out to be an idiot—but what an idiot! The story does not really begin until her arrival.

"If I scream for the butler I shall awaken my dear aunt, but I am dying of thirst." St. Cucuface climbed out of the sofa and went to the kitchen. He returned with a leftover half-bottle of champagne and glasses. He poured and then sank back again, keeping his eyes on the stairs as he talked.

"What I have told you up to now was simply by way of an overture. Now we begin with the miraculous story of Consuelo, the idiot child in the golden frame on the piano over there."

Klink, klank, klonck, klinkidiglinki glank klonk di klonk went the carillon, and then the hour sounded.

"Consuelo was the fourth child of her parents and the heiress to immense fortunes. She was a member of an American dynasty, so famous that it was impossible for them to put her into an institution or to keep her around. The family originally came from Bordeaux, which accounts for the interest in this locale. A representative called, the castle was inspected, the whole place was thoroughly gone over. The institutional white wall was built, modern plumbing was installed, the roof repaired, the lawn arranged, and the million-dollar asylum for the child was ready. I am told that even the garbage trucks had white-walled tires.

"In New York, friends of the family asked: 'Where is Jenny?' The answer was always: 'Oh, she's in the country,' and this answer was given until people stopped asking, and Jenny, who was renamed Consuelo, was indeed in the country, she was in

116

the gardens of the Château de Plaisir in the care of my Aunt Eulalia, who, I am happy to say, sincerely came to love the child.

"There is an album somewhere with a hundred-odd pictures of that period, all of them taken by Eulalia. And I need not tell you that the films and the camera, the equipment and the cows in the model dairy, in short, everything needed and all that could be anticipated, was provided by the family through a middleman, the public-relations counsel of the dynasty, a man called Asa Bullwinkle, who had suggested and engineered the plan. In the bulky contract that Mr. Bullwinkle had submitted for the signature of my aunt was an underlined clause stipulating that all visitors to the castle were to be cleared through his office. Excepted from this ruling were the immediate staff, a Paris doctor, and the Curé de St. Cucugnan, whose church had been restored by the mysterious benefactors across the ocean.

"The secret of the Château de Plaisir was well kept; the legend that ran through the gossip mills here was that Eulalia had inherited a vast fortune from an Italian uncle who had emigrated to Brazil.

"The child grew, and at the age of fourteen she looked like a young woman.

"Gossip had taken all this time to reach the Duke de Milfuegos in New York, where he had sustained life as a wine salesman, living under the incognito of Alfonso de Figueras. When he heard of the happy change in Eulalia's fortunes, he composed the first of a series of letters to her. In them, he pictured himself as lonesome and filled with the deepest remorse. He fanned the embers of their old love and even wrote a poem—he composed *Liebeslieder* in the mood of Schumann—

117

and spaced his Weltschmerz-laden communications so as not to seem unduly hasty. In fact, he was most careful not to reveal his knowledge of the great changes at the Château de Plaisir. He wrote of a simple plan for their life together — 'Now that we have become sensible.'

"Poor Eulalia allowed herself to be persuaded. She submitted the Duke's name to Mr. Bullwinkle, and after it had been cleared, she wrote him that she looked forward to his visit.

"He borrowed the money and one day the electric, patented, automatic American lock clicked, and the iron gates of the Château de Plaisir swung open upon the taxi that carried the Duke de Milfuegos, arriving for an extended visit."

Klunk klank klinking klunk klinkiðiklinkink klunk klunk klunk.

"He rubbed his hands in front of the fire there, he walked up and down the newly carpeted halls, he sat here, where we are, and drank wine out of these glasses, and he could now appreciate all these things better than ever before.

"In the beginning he had played the surprised man to perfection. And then, when the chill of the hard world from which he had come went out of him, he began to feel at home. He stroked his mustache, he hovered about my bulky aunt in poses of gallantry and adoration, shaking his head again and again, in seeming unbelief at her great fortune. The *dea ex machina* of the play, Consuelo, he had glimpsed only occasionally and at a distance as she walked to or from the castle.

"After the candles had burned down during another good dinner and the glasses were emptied and the kind Eulalia rose from the table in order that the butler could clear off the table and go to bed, they came as usual into this room, where my aunt loved to play the piano after dinner. She sat down and had struck a few chords, and the Duke was comfortably arranged listening, when the good Eulalia felt that here, at last, was the one person whom she could trust completely. She stopped after playing but one of his *Liebeslieder*, poured him more brandy and some for herself, as she sat down next to him.

"He patted her hand and kissed it, and then her cheek. Gratefully she clasped his thin hand on which the veins stood out like the ribs on autumn leaves. She took his head in her warm hands and kissed him on the lips, and he rallied sufficiently to recognize this as the proper moment to ask her to marry him.

"He had said the first few words, when Eulalia stopped him, and swearing him to silence, confided the secret of the Château de Plaisir to him. Together with the disclosure of the source of her wealth came the information that their marriage was subject to the consent of Mr. Bullwinkle. That is, their marriage and life at the Château de Plaisir. Their marriage, elsewhere — the simple, sensible life of which he had written and for which she was more than ready to forgo the luxuries of this million-dollar sanitarium — was of course a matter subject only to the good offices of the Curé de St. Cucugnan, and could indeed be arranged tomorrow.

"The Duke de Milfuegos was wide awake now. He finished the rest of the old brandy that night.

"'What are you thinking about?' asked Eulalia.

"'I am thinking about what is the best thing to do,' he said truthfully."

Klinkidiklank klunk klunk — Klank klank klinkidiklunk.

8.

Consuelo

"MATTERS ARE always difficult for a man who is not a complete cad. The astonished Duke felt that now he was indeed the stepchild of Fate. He had committed himself to the position of guardianship of an idiot. He would be the employee of Asa Bullwinkle, a condition worse than being a wine salesman. He was dependent upon the generosity of the Americans—the last was the one thing he consoled himself about, by saying, 'Who isn't?'

"In his confusion he took time out. He sat and twirled the ends of his mustache, crossed and recrossed his legs and then ran around, re-examining the property, inside and out, and carefully taking stock of installations, of the cows, the employees (for in that succession things were arranged in his feudal mind). He weighed all the comforts carefully, particularly the central heating system, the electric walk-in iceboxes, and the swimming pool; the storage room with the vast boxes of supplies that came regularly from America. 'Nothing like it in the whole of France,' the foreman had said as he unpacked the new ice-cream freezer.

"The Duke lay tossing for two nights and during the day he was pacing the court of honor beneath the mighty oak. On the third day he finally saw things clearly.

"That night after the dinner hour, when the candles were burning low again, and the old servant that you have seen, the deaf one who was robust then, cleared off and said good night and the Angel Eulalia went to the music room and leafed through the *Liebeslieder,* he came and for a while he halfheartedly accompanied her on the flute.

"The fragments of the frail goblet of their happiness that had been assembled with care and patience, and were almost ready to be glued, now seemed to be ready for the dustpan. She was pale and frightened, singing one of his songs. At the end of it, he abruptly asked the question on which he had anchored his plans.

"'But what will become of the child?' he said. And so cow dumb is a woman in love and so boarded up her vision that Eulalia took this as proof of his gentle nature. She called herself happy. 'Come and let me embrace you,' she said. Her beloved was indeed worth all the anguish and the time lost, for he was truly noble. 'You are good, you are kind and you are a saint, dearest—you are my own true love.' She was at last certain of complete happiness now, the path was smooth, the pieces were glued together, they would drink from the goblet at last. The Duke was so surprised by Eulalia's reaction that he dropped the flute. It broke—you can see it—it hangs there next to her portrait held together by a ribbon.

"The child had been on Eulalia's conscience—she was responsible for her, the only human being that Consuelo recognized. Eulalia telephoned early the next morning and instructed the nurse to bring Consuelo. Until then, with consideration for the Duke as well as for her, the child had been led the length of her dull day along paths that didn't cross his.

"The idiot was brought into this room. She looked at Milfuegos with her immense beautiful eyes and he walked over and kissed her on the eyes, on the temples and the forehead, and he held both her hands in his and kissed them; and suddenly tears rolled down her cheeks, and as he embraced her and stroked her hair, everyone in the room was weeping.

"From that day on, he took the greatest pains with her, he walked with her, pointed at objects in nature, slowly pronouncing their names. He fed her, he brushed her hair and Eulalia says that every day he prayed for her in the private chapel of the castle. He now was in a state of grace, and all the people of the Château de Plaisir were glad of his being there. It had been impossible until then to make Consuelo move, or to make her speak—or eat by herself. She was mostly in a mood of mute despair. With staring eyes she stood or sat where she was placed; the urges of the millions of years that are in our blood and bones had made pause in her. She lived and breathed as an automaton and her heartbeat was only a little below normal.

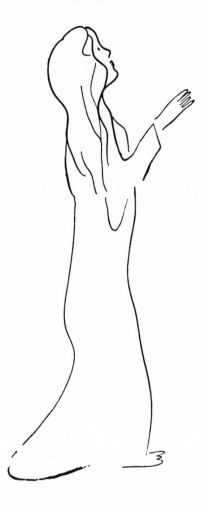

From the mutism in which she was most of the time, she fell periodically into a deep trance, which was accompanied by swelling of her face—she seemed then catapulted back past the animals to clay and was an immobile, dormant bed patient for weeks. This changed to a mood of maniacal excitement in which she played all the discords possible on the shrill two-stringed instrument that was her voice.

"Between the two extremes was a calm period, in which she was happiest and most beautiful. During this cycle, she wandered about freely—sometimes at night, addressing herself in mimicry to the trees, to the stars, to shafts of moonlight—and she danced in the light and to the playing of the carillon, accompanying it with small animal sounds of pleasure.

"It was an arduous task but a labor of love. In two years Milfuegos, the patient spider, had succeeded in attaching a thin, silken thread to the soul of Consuelo. He had incessantly bombarded the lump of clay until it secreted a drop—and this precious liquid ran along the thread into his hand: it was a smile of recognition. An idiot's smile, but with it a thousand tons of shale were lifted. It was a miracle, and soon followed by another; the birth of her first thought: she answered him. And as the *Viecherl* had crawled slowly from the fireplace, awakened by the music of Schumann, so now Consuelo was awakened from her long winter sleep by the kind ministrations of the good Duke.

"Her words were heavy, like stones, and one felt that they were lifted to her mouth with a great effort. She was able to speak only when her large beautiful eyes could steadily bathe in his own.

"'Consuelo,' she said first, and then, 'Consuelo sings, Consuelo cries and sings her love—' Then one day, like a parrot, she suddenly repeated a whole conversation that she had heard, including some quite difficult words.

"She also used some rather coarse expressions that she had heard backstairs, her favorite being *salaud*.

"He was triumphant, and doubled his efforts. They had a favorite place, in a grove a half hour's distance from the castle.

He would take her there and spend an hour in the morning with his pupil. One day, as she stood before him in the sunlight, Consuelo suddenly lifted her dress, revealing herself completely nude beneath it. Her figure was pleasantly plump, strongly modeled calves, the portion from the knee to the pelvis well rounded, the torso of a French peasant girl—the body that one sees in Renoir's pictures, voluptuous and warm.

"He told my aunt of the incident and the nurse was called in and reprimanded for not dressing the child properly. It was learned then that Consuelo had on that day and for the first time completely dressed herself. The Duke had mildly reproached the child, and the stupid governess, now having access to her mind, had frightened her with a ghost story such as are told to make children behave. Her progress was halted and she sat immobile, seeming to fall back into the old pattern of indifference. The governess was discharged and after patient efforts the Duke succeeded once more in awakening her; but now she had a fear of people, and particularly of sorcerers and ghosts. One must remember that her family came originally from Bordeaux and that it is only three centuries ago that five hundred sorcerers were put to death by fire in that city by order of the court. The Duke redoubled his efforts and eventually she hurdled this, the last obstacle, for now she breathed freely again and broke the last of her bonds. She was then sixteen.

"She sat up, she walked, she ran, her body became lithe, and her mind turned itself upon a world which she observed with freshness and audacity. Once looking at a fox terrier Consuelo said, 'Why do they always have black spots and never white?' It was a profound observation and I have never since that time looked at a fox terrier without thinking of her. Many of the things she said were worthy of being perpetuated on luxurious paper.

"The selfless Eulalia often thanked God for having brought the good Duke back to the isolation of her castle.

"She was patient. She spent much time in the chapel hoping that the cure would soon be complete, for once free from his arduous task, her beloved would find time to bother about her. In the meantime she was humbly grateful that he was near.

"The Duke, his plans complete in every detail, was constantly with his pupil; occasionally he looked at Eulalia with sadness, the sadness with which one looks upon a sheep that will be slaughtered soon. The innocent Eulalia mistook it for love.

"The only one worried at all about the astonishing progress of Consuelo was Mr. Bullwinkle, who would be faced with grave problems if what he read in the glowing letters from the Château de Plaisir were true.

"It appeared that he would have to deal with this miracle cure with a public-relations miracle of his own. It was a situation fraught with most delicate problems and awful possibilities. Asa Bullwinkle picked up the phone in his Philadelphia office, and inquired about sailing dates.

"The Duke now set more difficult problems for his pupil. He sat in the lilac grove looking at her, preparing her for the world she would eventually live in, which he had decided would be the appropriate climate for an heiress: the *beau monde* of America.

" 'Consuelo.'

" 'Yes, my dear.'

" 'Repeat after me — "simply divine." '

" 'Simply divine,' repeated Consuelo.

"'Say it with exaltation as if it meant something very important to you.'

"'*Si*mply di*vine.*'

"'Very good. Now repeat after me: "I'm having a perfectly wonderful time." '

"'Also important?'

"'Yes, Consuelo, very important.'

"'I've had such a good time.'

"'All right, if you want to say it your own way. Repeat it.'

"'I've had such a good time.'

"'Very good. Now when you say it, incline your beautiful face, dear, and look at me, the eyes wholly given to the words.'

"'I've had such a good time.'

"'Perfect. Now let's try "out of this world." Look up at the ceiling for an instant when you say that.'

"'Out of this world,' said Consuelo, swinging her eyes upward.

"'That is enough for today,' said the Duke. 'I'm very proud of you.'

"The Duke had persuaded Eulalia to purchase a dogcart and a horse, and with this he took Consuelo on drives through the neighborhood, extending her acquaintance with her environment.

"Now there is no actual proof, and the Duke cannot be accused, but looking back on it, Eulalia, with a bitter insistence on detail, remembers that although it was midsummer, there were always two folded woolen blankets on the seats of the cart. When properly driven, 'the whip,' as the driver of such an equipage is called, merely puts on a foot mantle, an apron of covert cloth which covers the legs. She remembers also that

Consuelo sometimes came back from the ride in a pleasant trance, contentment shining in her soft eyes. Once Eulalia heard her say as she stepped out of the cart, 'I've had such a good time, you *salaud*.'

"My poor aunt is now convinced that the most intimate embraces had been part of the Duke's therapy and that he had broken the paralysis by leading Consuelo over the tantalizing and exciting paths of the Garden of Love.

"She became alarmed about that time but blamed her fears on her own suspicious nature. It was about then that Mr. Asa Bullwinkle announced his impending arrival. When he learned of this, the Duke took to pacing the red-tiled courtyard again. He began teaching in a sharply accelerated tempo, and equipped her with four more phrases, which she learned in the week that Mr. Bullwinkle spent aboard a luxurious ocean liner, the owners of which were also among his clients."

Klunk klank, klinkiðiklink klunk klaaaaaaank.

9·

Escapade

"THERE WAS no need to open the automatic electric gate for Asa Bullwinkle, for he swooped down out of the sky in a small plane and emerged from it in front of the castle.

"Mr. Bullwinkle was as modern in his mode of travel as he was antique in dress. He went to the door of the castle and entering, placed his yellow gloves and the cane together with the Churchill hat on the Spanish commode in the hall and proceeded to follow the sound of moaning which came from this room.

"He found poor Eulalia dissolved in tears, for she had just

that moment discovered that the Duke had disappeared with his pupil.

"The Curé de St. Cucugnan had telephoned that upon rising, and while looking at the weather out of the window, his housekeeper had observed the Duke tying the horse to the hitching post in front of the tavern across from the church; that the Duke then had lifted Consuelo out of the cart and taken from it two traveling bags. The housekeeper had run to the church and told him, but there was a delay and he had been unable to report this immediately, first because the housekeeper had to wait to tell him since he had been in the middle of morning Mass, second because there was no telephone in the rectory. As soon as possible he had gone to the nearest telephone, which was at the post office, and from there had made his report. The horse and cart were still in Cucugnan. The Duke, Consuelo and the baggage were gone.

"Mr. Bullwinkle let out an animal cry of anguish. His mousetail mustaches quivered as he yelled at poor Eulalia: 'It's you that is the idiot!' He paced the floor, he suffered intense agonies and heaped upon himself the most stinging professional rebukes. His dilemma was manifold. Since there had been so much secrecy regarding the child ever since her earliest years, only the most discreet inquiries about her whereabouts were possible; the aid of the police and the press could not be enlisted, for ironically enough, Bullwinkle, the specialist in making unpleasant facts about his clients palatable to the public, now found himself working without the tools whose use he knew better than any other man in his trade. He must abstain from telephoning, telegraphing, dictating, writing, issuing bulletins and arranging press conferences. After his first outburst Asa Bullwinkle sank into a torpor and collapsed on this sofa for an hour—the longest relaxation he had ever given himself in years.

"He ordered a car and when it came, drove to the village of Cucugnan, where he made frantic inquiries. He was informed that the Duke had bought two tickets to Nîmes, which is forty-five kilometers from Cucugnan. From there they might have gone to Paris, to Italy or Spain, or anywhere, for that matter.

"Mr. Bullwinkle returned to the castle. He found Eulalia in a new bath of tears and the butler just bringing in a birthday cake with seventeen candles. *Consuelo* was written in pink icing across the white center. And the Duke's coat of arms appeared on a shield of sugar attached to the side of the cake.

"At the sight of it, my poor aunt cried, 'Take it away—take it out, for the love of God, and leave me alone. I want to die.'

"Mr. Bullwinkle was beginning to function again. 'That sonofabitch knows exactly what he's doing,' he said, looking at the cake. 'We shall hear from him eventually.'

"He wrote down his Paris address for my aunt and told her that if word should come, she was to get in touch with him immediately. In the meantime, life at the Château de Plaisir was to continue exactly as if Consuelo were still there. There were to be no more visitors, and no telephone calls except to him. Mr. Bullwinkle put on his hat and gloves and boarded his plane. He rushed back to Paris and waited a week, but there was no message. He sailed for America to inform his clients of the unhappy state of affairs at the Château de Plaisir.

"Except for a moment's sadness when she had heard the

distant *klink klank klunk* of the carillon as they drove to the station, the Duke and his pupil were radiantly happy as they traveled to Marseilles.

"She entertained him with the observations of her newly acquired and highly original mind. He had taught her a small ritual of saying 'I do' when a priest asked her a question; he had rehearsed the marriage ceremony as performed in Catholic churches in France with her, the chambermaid and the porter of their hotel assisting. After the required three days of waiting, Consuelo became the Duchess of Milfuegos in the Basilica of Notre Dame de la Gare, a small soot-covered place provided for the devotions of railroad employees.

"The Duke had been most careful in his planning, and they obtained rooms in an obscure tavern, the Hôtel des Voyageurs, and that is where Consuelo saw her first elephant. She was looking out of their third-story window, watching the animal as it was helping to unload a circus in the local freight yard.

"She was nearly beside herself with happiness, continually pointing at the wonderful things that came out of the cars on the tracks across the way, and in a voice that had now become melodious, she called him constantly to the window to share her pleasure.

"The evening of the third day, as man and wife, but with the Duke traveling under his wine merchant's incognito of Alfonso de Figueras, and with his mustache trimmed, they left the hotel and boarded the steamer *Breteuil.*

"Consuelo again said something profound, this time to the captain of the ship—the first ship she ever remembered seeing. She stood on the bridge and pointed forward to the bow and asked, 'Is this always the front of the ship?'

132

"No one had ever asked that question of the captain before. He took off his cap and scratched his head in bewilderment. 'No, not always.' Since he was at that moment engaged in backing the vessel out of the slip, it seemed the only reply.

"Once they were under way, the Duke relaxed and from then on made no great effort to further educate Consuelo. Patiently he awaited the birth of their child, which was perfectly normal and which was quite as much a joy and a surprise to the Duchess as the elephant had been. After the infant had been baptized, the Duke disclosed his whereabouts in a businesslike communication to Asa Bullwinkle. He politely asked for information about the will of the founder of the dynasty, as it concerned the great-granddaughter, the Duchess of Milfuegos, and her son, the Dauphin Alfonsito.

"Again publicity and scandal were discreetly avoided. Mr. Bullwinkle boarded a plane and forty-three hours later was installed in a suite at Shepheard's Hotel. While the Duchess played with her baby son, the Duke and the public-relations counsellor sat down together. They very quickly came to an understanding. In fact, the disclosures of Asa Bullwinkle exceeded the Duke's most reckless estimates.

"'Mr. Bullwinkle, you are a most understanding man,' he said.

"Mr. Bullwinkle returned the compliment.

"The Duke was surprised to learn that the visitor knew a good restaurant in Cairo of which he had not heard, and they repaired there to continue their conversation at luncheon. It was very much like one of the many conference-lunches which were routine with Mr. Bullwinkle in New York.

"The Duke had outlined his plan on a sheet of green paper,

and his calculations were made in tiny figures, barely readable, and he had in a very orderly fashion added up the various columns. (It should be said that these demands included a pension to be paid to Eulalia, which would enable her to continue living in modest circumstances at her castle.)

"He produced this instrument with the coffee and Mr. Bullwinkle gave it a quick reading, the elongated ends of his mustaches quivering as he read.

"Finally he lit a cigar and said with a smile, 'We'll do better than that, better by a wide margin.' With that he handed the green paper back to the bewildered Duke and he began to outline a plan, conceived in the most openhanded generosity, a plan which included all concerned and also himself, for he explained that it would be in the best interests of his clients that he take care of the affairs of the Duke.

"'We are like two vast circles touching,' said Mr. Bullwinkle eloquently.

"'Our only problem is to merge these two circles, so that only one will be visible.'

"It was a little confusing, like Consuelo's language, and the Duke stared for a while at Mr. Bullwinkle, hoping he might enlarge on this remark; but the public-relations specialist merely blew smoke rings and looked very pleased with himself; he was thinking he would take the Duke to lunch in New York, he would give a party at his house for him in Philadelphia; it would add to his prestige as well as to his retainer.

"He said that his services began with this day and that he had put funds at the Duke's immediate disposal.

"The Duke showed great self-restraint in not borrowing

some cash from his public-relations counsel then and there at the table.

"Mr. Bullwinkle had pulled an imposing wallet from his old-fashioned *pet-en-l'air* coat, and held it open as he waited for the bill. It was stuffed with American currency of high denominations and the Duke had trouble in keeping his eyes off it.

"The plane for Paris leaves Cairo at two, and the Duke, on the way back from the flying field, urged the driver to proceed with all possible speed to Barclay's Bank in order to get there before it closed. He arrived and the large check he presented there was honored. Since he was as capable of gratitude as he was of sentiment, the Duke sat down that night at the hotel and wrote one of the most beautiful letters that my Aunt Eulalia has ever received."

Kling klink klunk bong bong bong.

—

THE DRONE of St. Cucuface's conversation was suddenly interrupted by the alarm of the aunt's voice going off abovestairs.

"I must hurry with the end of the story," said St. Cucuface; "she's getting up.

"The Duke now lives the pleasant international life, and his happiness consists of putting a great deal of money into circulation.

"The Duchess is happy also. Occasionally she appears at the opera in an old pair of carpet slippers, but that is the fault of her maid, for she still must be told to put on her clothes garment by garment, beginning with girdle and stockings, and any negligence in that direction sometimes leads to an interesting effect.

"In New York, during the season, you may see her lunching or dining in the royal enclosure of all the best restaurants, and from the best tables that surround her come the heartiest hellos, the widest smiles, the nods and the gay waving of arms. 'How did you like the play last night?' one of the leaders of the coterie might shout to her across the carpet.

"At such a question, the Duchess usually inclines her lovely head and answers, 'Simply divine, I mean, really out of this world.'

"They have all accepted her as their own, she is a great success and none of them know that she is an idiot, or ever was."

The Count and I suddenly sat up straight. A fragment of an aria floated down from above. A door had been opened above and several of the fox terriers came running and falling down

136

the stairs. I realized that Consuelo's remark about the spots on them was profound and unforgettable.

Klinkety klink klunk klaannng.

We struggled out of the couch to our feet.

"In summing up," St. Cucuface said—"Isn't it wonderful that everything ends happily in this tale? The idiot lives happily outside of an asylum, the Duke without having to be a wine salesman, and my dear Aunt Eulalia without having a bounder for a husband."

"We will have a little repast now," said the Princess, as she entered the room, "and then we shall get ready to go to the party of my new neighbor, Monsieur Rosay."

She screamed for the butler and floated toward the combination radio and record player of American make, to get some news of the confused outside world.

10.

Masquerade

AN OLD FRIEND called for the Princess. He came in a vintage De Dion Bouton, a bus-like, chauffeur-driven phaeton so high it allowed the tall gallant to keep his top hat on.

We drove out of the court of honor of the Château de Plaisir (*Klunk, klank, klinkidiklink*) and down the straight road into the dark forest.

"My cousin Jean, or John as he prefers to be called, sold the château," said Cucuface. "He could no longer pay his help and there is nothing more depressing than a castle not properly kept up, or does one say upkept—

"If my old Uncle Hubert was '*vieille France*,' then my cousin Jean, or John as he prefers to be called, is oddly enough, 'old England.' John's mother was English and he married an English girl; they did not marry for love of each other, but because both were devoted to horses. The Countess hunted when she was *enceinte* and when her daughter was born a wicker saddle was ordered for her, and the stable was her nursery. She was given a hunter at an age when other little girls received dolls and her governess was an ancient retired cavalry sergeant from St. Cyr.

"She still speaks French with a British accent, and at ten years of age she would throw such phrases into the conversation as 'Came across a really smashing good mare today.'

"John should have been altogether English. As it was, he shipped his horses across the Channel; he became infatuated with the brandy faces over there and it was a pity that he couldn't have afforded to hunt with them really. *Mon Dieu*, it's contagious—I'm even talking like him now.

"The pale orchid silks of his jockeys were seen at all the English race meets; he rode well himself, no man sustained more falls, but his racing policy was somewhat eccentric. He was too cocksure of himself; once he accepted a bet of £10,000 to £110 half an hour before the race, and that time he won it. All in all, however, he lost. For a man half French, his poise in defeat was marvelous. His fortunes declined sharply, and he finally gave up racing and retired to hunting, still staying in England.

"Among people of quality he felt that he was the right man in the right place; but England changed, and quality went out; the sport became too costly for the lords, and he had no taste to hunt with a ragged lot. A few years ago, just before the war, he came back here with only one horse, his favorite. In the words of the child: 'A smashing good mare,' named Penelope.

"He was determined to make his country, and particularly this countryside, as much like England as possible. He arranged hunts and hunt balls. He detested soft living and comfortable furniture; he threw it all out and tore down the draperies, and he announced that he couldn't eat our cooking any more. He brought with him an old English servant, a bowlegged man in canvas puttees who was all bones and a good hand at turning out a chop and a cup of tea. The two of them remeasured the landscape here, substituting miles for kilometers—and in this, the worst scenting country in the world, John killed a dozen foxes in as many days.

"After his cup of tea and the chop, which he took for breakfast, he would ride fifty miles a day. He was an immense man. You must notice the chairs at Cucugnac: they were especially made for him. Normal people have to sit on the edge of them.

"He is past seventy now, as lively as a cricket, and when he lays down his horn for good, there will expire the last of his kind. I have known him for thirty years but never really well."

"APPARENTLY everybody who was invited has accepted Monsieur Rosay's invitation," said St. Cucuface as we came out of the forest and found that we had to slow down, there were so many cars in front of us.

"Look, Monsieur Rosay has made improvements. If poor John would see that, he'd lay down the hunting horn now," said Cucuface.

Up to the château led a row of fountains, brightly illuminated. Instead of water, there rose from bowls of modern stucco
cascades of silk. The various fabric fountains were identified by
luminous posters. We drove past such splendors as "Royal
Rosay," a dark crimson fabric; "Rose Rosay," strawberry-

colored silk; then white "Neige Rosay"; after that an aqua-marine fountain called "Isles Rosay," and an emerald one, "Niles Rosay." Again a flaming one, "Kiss Rosay," and now that we were near we could read that under the name of the fountain there was in smaller print certain additional information: under "Kiss Rosay" was printed "Don't hesitate." Under "Château Rosay" — "Invite me," etc.

Unnamed but by far the most stupendous were the last two fountains, which stood directly in front of the castle. These were made of various materials sprouting from golden bowls. The effect of foam was obtained by hundreds of ermine and white astrakhan pelts, thrown into the bowl to form a frothy base. The fountains shooting upward were made of pale blue damask covered with silver sequins, and six arches of pleated mother-of-pearl satin simulated the falling waters. In the daz-zling light of these two majestic and revolving fountains the guests stepped out of their cars. Footmen in white silk breeches guided them over a carpet of roses to a row of pillars wound in golden organdy.

Those who were in costume ascended the stairs to the castle. The others were ushered to a tent lined with "Rosay Ravis-sante," a lesser product of the mills of the host. Here was an assortment of costumes made of "Redoute Rosay," "Raillerie Rosay," "Masquerade Rosay," and other materials of shimmer-ing satin. While two maids and a make-up man were busy with us, a young lady stopped and smilingly held toward us a placard which said that these materials while of dazzling beauty were economically priced and were destined for costumes, for the space of one unforgettable night.

The theme of this unforgettable night was a *fiesta* in the palace of Mohammed Abdul Rosay. There was a pageant and needless to say, the wine served was *vin rosé* courtesy of the vintner whose credit line appeared in the silk-bound souvenir programs along with the name of the firm of electricians who flood-lighted the fountains. It also contained the names of the various patrons and the list of the guests. The center spread of the program was a group photograph of the most beautiful and famous models who had been brought from Paris to parade in Rosay creations.

"A very useful man to know if you need silk," said St. Cucuface as a turban was wound around his head.

We were dressed with the utmost care. Crackling and swishing out of the tent in our silks, satins and brocades, we saw spread before us a scene that could compare with anything the Grand Saison in Paris or ancient Egypt had ever provided in brilliance and elegance: the most beautiful costumes, the most beautiful women, the most interesting men.

If this night fell short of its promise it would not be the fault of Monsieur Rosay, whose name, emblazoned on a huge banner of silk, floated in a rose spotlight from the tower of the castle.

A footman was announcing the guests, music was playing, the stars shone from the ceiling of the ballroom. The guests were dancing to what sounded like a frenetic minuet; it was an American square dance, currently the rage in Paris, and this rustic capering was done by sheiks in flowing robes and ladies wearing some forty yards of white tulle.

"*Son Altesse, le Prince de Bavière,*" announced the butler. Madame Rosay, in a costume that looked like a dozen tasseled

lampshades and a pearl-studded Genghis Khan cap with emerald earflaps, curtsied low. Her daughter, in Oriental costume, curtsied.

"*Le Comte de St. Cucuface,*" said the butler. They bowed and we passed.

"I have to find out where is the buffet and where is my aunt and her group," said St. Cucuface, disappearing among the gay dancers.

Everyone here was important. Here were the great dressmakers, the famous publicity men, fashion people, American buyers and the aristocracy of the garment trade, who had given their great names to various products: here were the Lipstick Prince and the Perfume Countesses, the Mattress Marquis, the Dress-shield Duchess, all milling about in a state of exaltation.

St. Cucuface reappeared. "I have found them," he said. "They look like the statues of doom, each face a mask; they are shipwrecked in the notions-and-button department. I also know where the buffet is. Come."

We walked to the buffet, which was at least ninety feet long. Small cards announced the hot dogs as "satin-skinned Rosay," and the menu was as varied as the guests. There were glazed hams from Ardennes, Coulibiac of salmon; various soups, among them Bortsch and cold Vichyssoise—and with that the buffet offered goulash, cheese blintzes, herring in jelly, rollmops, gaffelbitters, saltsticks and pickles. The cloth on which the various dishes rested was of most modern weave, a super-rayon "with the durability of stainless steel, and may be cleaned by simply wiping with a moist cloth." The card on which this was lettered leaned against one of the ten candelabras that stood among the food.

St. Cucuface was busy fixing his first caviar and cold turkey sandwich. He then proceeded to stuff himself with it and with small babkas filled with truffles and goose livers. Then, wiping his hands and mouth on a Rosay napkin, he began to pile food on plates for his aunt and her friends.

With each of us carrying plates, followed by a footman with glasses and wine, we moved through the crowd to find the Princess. Following an arrow that said "Velvet Street," we came eventually to a room which St. Cucuface identified as a former library. The books had been removed and on the shelves stood velvet palettes bearing thousands of buttons.

In the center of the room hung a map which showed the empire of Monsieur Rosay. Made of varicolored cloth, it reached from ceiling to floor. The various branches of the House of Rosay were indicated on it — "*Paris, Lyon, Bordeaux, Lille, Marseille, Nice, Alger, Bruxelles, Londres, Milan, Genève, New-York, Buenos Aires, Rio de Janeiro, Santiago.*"

Beneath it was embroidered: "*Ask for our representative to call on you.*"

Grouped in front of the "Rosay Aquamarine" ocean were the Princess and her friends. They were sitting on bolts of cloth in attitudes of boredom.

The food and wine seemed to restore them. They ate with great appetite and we had to make four trips to the buffet before all of them were fed.

With the wine they discovered each other and began to talk with animation. They paired off, and two of them found out that they lived only two hours from one another and had not seen each other for twenty years — in fact each had counted the other as dead.

The most antiquated aristocrat of the lot, a marquis whose
yellowish white hair was heavily pomaded and parted in the
middle all the way down to the back of his neck, leaned toward
the feeble Baroness de la Tour Midi, who among all this cou-
turier's skill and glory looked as though she were dressed in a
fuchsia burlap bag, and the following conversation took place:

"Do you remember Mafalda Torricelli?"

"Ah, yes, poor dear, dead these two years."

"But, my dear, she was only sixty-eight—and how is
Ghibellini Torricelli?"

"Also dead."

"Good God—"

"Do you remember Lea? You know, the woman he was so
fond of?"

"Quite dead, my dear—"

"It's really frightening, isn't it? What about Claudia—?"

"She's here."

"My God, dead too, and Ettore?"

"He's here, too—"

"He's dead? Dear Ettore—he used to play at Cannes—is
dead?"

"No, I said he's *here*. Look to your right—"

"Oh, and what is he doing?"

"He is living on bridge, very high."

"How silly. What can you mean, living on a bridge? You
mean in Florence. He's not that bad off, I hope."

"I said *on bridge*, not on a bridge. On playing bridge."

"Oh, it's in the blood then, isn't it? Pity."

"Remember the baccarat scandal?"

"I am seventy-six, of course I remember it, who doesn't?"

They moved still closer together and the Marquis continued to shout:

"I will never forget it: Papa came home, and he repeated what the judge had said.

"The judge had asked the accused, 'Have you told this to your wife?'

"'Yes, I tell everything to my wife,' he had answered.

"'How very foolish,' said the judge.

"Well, you know he and Papa were great friends; and isn't it odd, only the other day I came across all the old scrapbooks, with the newspaper clippings of that time."

"I know and the very worst of the caricatures."

"And in an old, old copy of an illustrated review—a photograph of old St. Cucuface—and all the people concerned in the *affaire baccarat.*"

"He was so handsome, he was so gallant, every maître d'hôtel and all the mounted police in Paris wept when he died."

"The police?"

"By police, I mean the *Garde Républicaine;* you know, the ones that stand on the stairs of the Opera on gala nights and ride out to the races."

"Oh, yes, yes, I know what you mean. I was always against that sort of thing, though, making flunkeys of the Army. Do they still have them?"

"I am told more than ever."

"*Au fond*, France will never change; the people still want a king."

"Of course. Did you hear that the Comte de Paris is back?"

"In his castle?"

"No, d'Amboise is damaged. German artillery, you know.

The terrace there, between the chapel and the main house, it's virtually gone, but then it never was comfortable. You remember Charles VIII broke his head when he galloped in through the low stone portal."

"Ah, so where will he stay?"

"Oh, at some hotel of course, unless the administration of the Beaux Arts concerns itself with restoring d'Amboise; and I think that since they aren't Royalists, they'd do it only in order to take tourists there."

"If it comes to that, I prefer to have the state take my castle, tourists or not. You see the disgusting alternative here tonight."

"How very right you are, my dear."

The footman came with a bottle and he filled the glasses lifted up in trembling hands. There was a sudden roll of drums, and the conversation stopped. Old necks were craned toward the ballroom, where, on a circular runway, the beautiful models appeared in the Rosay silks and the latest creation of the *haute couture*.

At the end of the hour-long presentation, prizes were awarded, and the girl who had been chosen Miss Rosay was introduced and crowned. Afterwards, as at the circus, the runway ring was taken apart and hastily carried out by liveried footmen.

"I'll go and see if there is anything my aunt wants," said St. Cucuface and disappeared in the direction of the buffet.

It was hot and humid in the ballroom, and the dancing had started again. I went out on the terrace and sat on a comfortable outdoor *canapé* upholstered in a rain-and-sun-resistant Rosay material, called, I noted by its large label, "Rosay Solaire."

After a while a man, in sultan's robes, came out on the terrace

and wandered to where I sat. He addressed me in French, and asked if I minded his sitting down. When I answered him in French, he began speaking English and after I had said a few words in that language, he said: *"Aber Sie Sprechen auch Deutsch?"* When I replied in German in the affirmative, he asked, in English, whether I was a buyer from New York.

I told him I was a friend of one of his guests.

"I am your host, and my doctor," he said, suddenly clutching his robed stomach, "has forbidden me any excitement. I hope they don't stay too late."

Monsieur Rosay's face was the color of "Kiss Rosay." He handed me two cigars and spoke of general topics in three languages — in each of which he appeared to command a handy argot. His English struck a nostalgic note: the speech of the taxi

150

driver who takes you from the boat to your New York hotel. He could say "Christ Almighty" as perfectly as he said *"D'accord,"* rolling it low and taking pleasure in the word, when agreeing with someone. *"Wo kommst Du her"* he said as if he had arrived but yesterday from Saxony, a place, incidentally, where a great deal of yarn is spun.

He was the product of the modern age, a man whom you will see in the Beverly Hills Hotel on Monday, on Wednesday in the Cub Room of the Stork Club in New York, and on a transatlantic plane the next day, as much at home and surrounded by the same faces; you might see him at Maxim's at the Friday Gala and again in a train to Berlin, being greeted as an old friend by the conductor in the sleeping car.

He occasionally interrupted our conversation to sing out a "Hiya, Baby" to a passing girl, or take an order for a shipment from a guest, committing it to memory and agreeing to the terms by taking his cigar out from his mouth and uttering his perfectly pronounced *"D'accord."*

When a footman came out on the terrace, Monsieur Rosay whistled, and the man brought him a glass filled with a milky liquid—"to line my stomach," explained Monsieur Rosay.

"One thing I and my wife agree on," he said. "If suddenly either of us or Denise, that's my daughter, should feel really sick, we get on the next plane for America. Take my advice, don't ever put yourself in the hands of a French doctor."

He seemed to find it difficult to sit in one position for long; he twisted, he writhed, and seemed to make constant decisions as to what to do with himself. He was a small paunchy man with restless eyes and his most characteristic motions were a twist of the head to the right and then to the left, as if he had a stiff neck and wanted to put it right, and then an apprehensive look upward, as if he were expecting something to fall on him.

"This is the last party here. Everything you see here is coming down, the whole thing," he said. "I'm going to start tearing it down next week. Luckily it's not what is known as a National Monument. I looked into that before I bought it.

"I've got a lot of diversified interests: I've got a night club in Bordeaux, I own a restaurant in Bordeaux, and I'm thinking of branching out. Now this place I'm going to turn into a farm. You avoid the estate taxes, and besides, it's good for growing things; the land must have rested for a couple of hundred years. The barns and stables I'm going to let stand. I'll maybe put up a small bungalow, but all the rest goes. Changes your tax setup — you're a farmer.

"I looked around a long time for a place. I just wanted a place in the country. And so I start looking, and the moment people hear that, they all come breaking your door down. Suddenly the whole country is full of castles; every real-estate agent beats a path to your door. Châteaux here and châteaux there, on the Loire, on the Rhone, on a hill, in a valley, and you can have them at your own price. So I got in my car and looked at châteaux for a month. Some of them are classified as National Monuments, and you can't trust them; others are too big, some are too shot up by the Germans and the worst are those in which the Americans have made themselves at home. I got damned tired of it; most of them are just picturesque ruins and in all of them you'd have to repair the roofs and put in your own plumbing and heating.

"So I gave up, until one day a guy came in with a set of

pictures of this place and said he had what I wanted. I liked it the moment I looked at it.

"So I got all the details, and arranged to meet the owner—he turned out to be an old guy, you know, a C. Aubrey Smith type, in a hunting coat, and white whiskers, and boots. So he showed me the house, and I went along, checking the inventory. And every few feet he stopped to reminisce. 'In this hall,' he said, 'my daughter's debut took place. There were over a hundred guests. She came down these stairs; the music was over there, and here was the receiving bower—' and then he walked around with me, and I asked if the china that hung on the wall went with the place. A lot of large platters with hunting scenes on them, very valuable stuff, I guess, collectors' items, you know. Well, the old guy said yes; he said, 'You'll find them listed in the inventory. Take 'em, take everything but my clothes and my boots,' he said. So we went out and he showed me the servants' quarters, and then we went down to the stable, down there to the left, and all tiled and neat. In one of the boxes was a horse, her name was Penelope; the nameplate is still up there.

"'Does the horse go with the place?' I asked him.

"He didn't talk for a while. He took off a glove and passed his hand over the horse's face. Then he said, 'No. The horse doesn't go with the place.'

"I said, 'My daughter knows how to ride, and so does my wife, and I could learn. As a matter of fact,' I said, 'the exercise would do me good.'

"He just said, 'No.'

"I said, 'I thought I got everything but the personal belongings.'

"He didn't give me any answer. He just stood there patting the horse, like before, and then without turning around, he said, 'Do you want the château or not?'

"So I said all right. 'Keep the horse,' I said.

"'We'll go back to the house then,' he said.

"So I started back.

"'I'll be with you in a second,' he said.

"So I walked up the hill, and then suddenly I heard a shot and I ran back, as fast as I could—and you know what that dumb old S.O.B. had done? He'd shot his own horse."

11.

The Calendar Man

WE LEFT EARLY in the morning after the Rosay party, for it was high time that we delivered her car to Madame l'Ambassadrice in Cannes. As it had been on our arrival, the Forêt de St. Cucuface was fogbound, and in the middle of it we met an old horse; and then the governess cart that the Princess had bought for Consuelo emerged from the white soup. It was bringing the morning mail, along with some boxes with American labels and Air Express tags.

The road from Montpellier to Toulon is, for the most part, as straight as a pencil. We drove as far as St. Tropez that day, and stopped to swim and eat. Cucuface called Cannes and engaged rooms at the new Grand Hôtel des Horizons, where we arrived without incident early the next day, that is, early on the Riviera, for it was exactly nine when we arrived.

Signor Stuzzicadenti, the Italian director of the palatial hotel, flanked by his assistant and a reception committee of doormen, footmen and bellboys, descended the onyx-and-marble stairs, and like a well-oiled teletype machine ran off his phrases of greeting. In his eagerness, he did a little dance in place, tapping his elegant Italian shoes, his dark eyes as busy as his lips and feet. He looked from our faces to the car and then into the plate glass window of the hotel lobby, where he checked the set of his gray morning coat and the pearl-colored four-in-hand tie. Below us was a sequence of little, tight-fitting, flower-crammed gardens which filled in the spaces between the snow-white decorative stairs, the winding walks, the fountains and driveways which led to the tennis courts, the swimming pool, and the parking lot in which, fender to fender, stood Alfa Romeos, Daimlers, Bentleys and Cadillacs.

Three elderly South American ladies in white were taking the early sun in chairs placed under a magnificent tropical tree whose branches rose to the third story of the hotel. "*Buenos días, buenos días, buenos días,*" the Director said carefully in their direction. He gave a "*Bon jour, Excellence,*" to a stout man with a large wart on his nose whom I recognized as a French industrialist, and called a friendly hello to a young woman in abbreviated shorts and dirty white sneakers who was running down to the tennis courts swinging her racket. "*Hélas,* they are the fashion now," he said. "Dirty sneakers are a vogue imported by our young American visitors. I have even been told that in

America the shoes are sold already especially dirtied. At any rate, it's the latest thing here. Our valets have strict orders never to clean them." I became aware of the hum of airplane motors, and the Director froze like a pointer in the field. Exactly over the center of the hotel, between its delicate white and azure towers, over the sign with the golden words GRAND HÔTEL DES HORIZONS attached to the artful modern meshwork which imitates the shape and color of the waves of the Mediterranean, there intruded the nacelle, the wings with the four motors, and then the rudder of a silver Constellation bearing the insignia of Air France.

Signor Stuzzicadenti stamped his foot.

"Here we have indeed achieved the hotel of hotels. There is none like it, not in the whole of this world; and every morning at this hour, when my guests are still asleep, this plane comes over the roof flying so low that one can overhear the conversation in the cabin."

"But isn't there something you can do about it?" asked St. Cucuface.

"Monsieur le Comte, I have been to the President of the Society of Hôteliers, the local Chamber of Commerce, the Syndicate of Initiative—all without avail. The only way to get rid of this nuisance is to mount a Bofors gun on the roof and shoot it down." He shook both fists after the plane, the tail of which was disappearing through the branches of the tall tropical tree under which the Brazilian ladies were resting. He smiled at them dutifully.

"A thousand pardons," said Signor Stuzzicadenti, remembering his manners. "Everything is ready; I've moved some people out, Altesse, and Monsieur le Comte, to give you the very best possible accommodations." He pointed at the first floor terrace: "Two bedrooms, each with its own terrace, bath and shower and a salon." The manager clapped his hands. *"Allez,"* he snapped, and the doorman, who had been standing stiffly by as at a military ceremony, saluted and smiled. He directed the unloading of the car by two page boys, dressed as he in heavenly blue, and — as all things in this hotel — brand new, fresh of face, elastic of step, the thirty-six buttons of their tight jackets sparkling in the Mediterranean sunshine.

"I shall arrange for the car to be washed and checked. When does the Prince desire it again?" the doorman asked, cap in hand.

"It's not His Highness's car," said St. Cucuface, and explained that it belonged to Madame l'Ambassadrice and that all charges connected with it were to be put on her bill.

"Oh," said the manager.

"Is there anything wrong?" asked St. Cucuface.

"Non," said Stuzzicadenti. "No, Monsieur le Comte. Except that it was the Ambassador and Madame whom we moved out in order to make room for you."

"Did they object?" asked St. Cucuface, as though to do so would have been patently unreasonable.

"Yes," said Stuzzicadenti. "Madame objected very strenuously. They are not too comfortable, I am afraid. I had to move them up, into a suite with a beautiful view, but only one bath. There are two rooms, connecting, but one bath only."

St. Cucuface began taking off his gloves, and this gesture of impatience ended the discussion and started the manager and his staff on the various details of getting us established.

There are no stairs in this hotel, but only ramps, and the

rooms look out upon the sea. The terraces are set at a slant, so that the banisters do not obstruct the view, and the underside of the terrace above is painted in green and white stripes, which give the effect of an awning overhead. This magnificent hostelry is perched upon the rocks a few miles outside the rumpus of Cannes, isolated in the costly seclusion of a moon-shaped promontory called *Le Rocher de la Lune*.

"You have never met the Ambassador?" St. Cucuface asked me.

"No."

"People here, you understand, are inclined to be amused by American men of affairs, but Mr. Fruehauf is an extraordinary man, as ambassadors go; not at all what you expect. For one thing, a man who cares nothing for protocol, or striped trousers or the Homburg.

"What I mean to say is, that in spite of all that, the husband of Madame l'Ambassadrice, a plain businessman, is an outstanding ambassador; he gets things done. I recommend him to you."

The valet had come to unpack, and I made a new discovery.

All the bathtubs I have ever known give one a cold shock as one leans against the porcelain. The perfection of the Grand Hôtel des Horizons was again evident in the tub: it was shockproof, it was of a pleasant, appropriate body temperature all over.

At noon the terrace was filled with guests. Madame l'Ambassadrice at once sighted St. Cucuface; she pressed him to her bosom and kissed him lingeringly. Beside her stood the Ambassador.

He had an immense cigar in an immense face. His voice was rich, his handclasp strong without being painful, and he weighed about two hundred and sixty pounds. He moved with the awkward shuffling of a bear, but a distinguished bear, an amiable bear, and a bear that wanted to be liked.

Madame l'Ambassadrice announced that she wanted to visit the Casino for her afternoon gambling.

"I left my system upstairs," she said to the Ambassador, her eyes snapping.

"You just stay here, dear, and I'll go and get it," said the Ambassador.

She sent a hard look after him. "We're living practically in the attic," she said. Then she smiled at St. Cucuface and said, "But otherwise it's great fun. Have you read the papers? I lost a million and a half francs last night. Of course that's nothing;

Farouk lost ten times that much, and the man who won it simply dropped dead, dead as a mackerel."

The Ambassador returned with a bundle of papers, held together by a rubber band, on which Madame had charted the next plays in her system. He carefully put them in his inside coat pocket and then, with the light soft step of the very big man, he moved toward the door, smiling benignly at the page boys on duty along the way. He waited outside with his wife's sables over his arm. The newly washed Rolls was brought up, and they set off for the Casino to play.

The next day the Ambassador and Madame l'Ambassadrice sat with us on the hotel terrace. The Bikini beauties were splashing in the pool and St. Cucuface idly pointed out various celebrities to Madame. The Ambassador was telling me the story of his life. We had covered the early struggles of his youth and had gotten as far as St. Paul, a place situated, he informed me, in a larger place called Minnesota. "It was then that I had my first big success," he said, smiling in recollection. He was interrupted at this point by his wife, who had overheard him. She turned from pointing out Ali, Rita and Schiaparelli and said sharply, "You might remember that there is a little word, called *we*." The Ambassador said, "Yes, dear, I'm sorry," and turning to me, he patiently began to retell the story of the acquisition of his first forest and his first paper mill, saying, "And then we—" "That's better," she said. "Oh, there's Orson, and the man in the blue trunks with the blonde, who is that?"

"Tyrone Power," said St. Cucuface. "Of the audible cinema."

"Well, now, let me tell you how we got into the calendar business," said the Ambassador.

161

"I can't imagine that the Prince can be very interested in bags and calendars," said Madame l'Ambassadrice in her macaw's voice.

The Ambassador appeared downcast. "I suppose to an outsider—" he began and began fumbling for a match.

When I said that I was interested, he moved his chair closer and offered me a cigar and within the next minutes extended to me a hearty invitation to visit his vast lumber empire. His face glowed as he said, "In November, that's when I hope you can be there; that's when we have our big get-together, out in St. Paul. What a time!" His large benevolent face wobbled with joy as he shook his head.

Madame left us, and with her St. Cucuface, who had promised to introduce her to the Marquis de Cuevas.

The instant Madame l'Ambassadrice had gone, as if kept in a pocket, like an extra cigar, a thin little man popped up from nowhere and took a seat next to the Ambassador. It was clear that this gentleman's presence was not tolerated while Madame was about. He had a sharp face with a plow of a nose, and a humorous mouth, which smiled at the Ambassador with affection and respect, and promptly ordered a drink. The little man's name was Mr. Tannenbaum.

"Very glad, delighted, to shake hands with a Prince." I shook his hand. It was like grasping the foot of a dead chicken.

He seemed cold all over. The boss said he'd have an old-fashioned.

"This man likes calendars," said the Ambassador, nodding in my direction.

"Is that so? Well, I tell you, Mr. Fruehauf here is the Calendar King, the King of the Calendar people—the famous

Fruehauf, Incorporated—twenty million calendars a year, and paper bags besides. They run into astronomical figures. Did anybody ever count how many paper bags we turn out a year, Mr. Fruehauf?"

"Billions of 'em," said Mr. Fruehauf, lifting his old-fashioned in his large hand.

"Now, Mr. Fruehauf here, there isn't a hotel he stays at or a ship or a train or a plane that he goes on, that he doesn't right off inspect the paper."

"That's right," said Mr. Fruehauf, looking modestly down at his cigar.

Mr. Fruehauf spoke freely now and only occasionally, when he was at loss for a word, did Mr. Tannenbaum have to come to his aid, as a lawyer leads a witness along in his testimony.

"When he comes back from a trip, Mr. Fruehauf here, why it's the same like a salesman taking to the road—only Mr. Fruehauf here, he brings back the samples. If it'd interest you, Prince, he's got a big trunk upstairs filled with them," said Mr. Tannenbaum. "Letterheads, paper bags, all kinds of calendars, tags, ancient paper, rag paper, blotters, stickers—anything that concerns papers, anything made of paper, down to funny hats and streamers."

During this recital, Mr. Fruehauf would occasionally nod and remark: "That's right."

Mr. Tannenbaum looked carefully in the direction in which Madame l'Ambassadrice had disappeared and then called the waiter. "I think I'll have another one. Won't you join us?" He stretched himself and I saw that he was wearing an embossed leather belt with a silver buckle.

A full-blown blonde in a Bikini passed by.

"Now that for example, we might use—or what would you say, Mr. Fruehauf?"

"Definitely not," said the Ambassador.

"You see, there are laws to calendar art," said Mr. Tannenbaum. "Now, we'd dress her more and at the same time dress her less, if you know what I mean. We'd maybe put her in a transparent nightie. There's about a hundred rules like that." The drinks came, the Ambassador began working on his immediately and Mr. Tannenbaum continued the lesson.

"The first rule is: It's gotta be a girl. And our experience has taught us that she mustn't ever be shown from the back. Second in importance, I'd say, are animals; that is, like a dog, preferably a puppy. Preferably a white puppy. Preferably a white woolly puppy with a black spot on the right side of its face."

"That's right. Over the eye," said the Ambassador.

"What's the third rule?"

"Feet," said Mr. Tannenbaum.

"Now you wouldn't think that such a thing entered into the picture—well, I tell you, it does." Mr. Tannenbaum came close. "Now a foot, when you show it naked, is very good, it's O.K., but it mustn't have five toes. You can show three and maybe you'll get by with four. But not five. Under no circumstances five."

Mr. Fruehauf had leaned back and appeared a little disturbed at the turn of the conversation. He looked around as if to see if anyone were listening. I noticed that he also wore a cowboy belt with a silver buckle.

"Do you belong to some kind of an organization that wears these belts?" I asked.

They both seemed to welcome this question. If they had been identical twins, the smiles of contentment that broke out on each face could not have been more alike.

"I can answer that," said Mr. Tannenbaum. The Ambassador looked proudly down at his buckle.

"Loyalty," he said, with closed eyes. "Loyalty to Mr. Fruehauf. This is the Fruehauf Belt, the famous Fruehauf Loyalty Belt that holds together the greatest bunch of guys in the world."

"I would be very happy to send you one," said the Ambassador. He lit a fresh cigar and waved the match in the air to extinguish it. "Shall I tell him about our annual get-together?"

"Sure—tell him."

"Well, I have this ranch in New Mexico, and every year, in November, we have a get-together of all the calendar people from all over the country. It's a very simple place—"

"He's kidding," said Mr. Tannenbaum. "I tell you, he's kidding you. It's the biggest ranch you ever saw: thousands of acres. And that's where, every year in November, we have this great big get-together of all the gang. Well, in the ranch house, the main house, that is, there's a room all decorated in gold, and that's where the boss here, Mr. Fruehauf, receives the delegates. And every one of 'em has one of these belts. And pretty important things are decided at these get-togethers, like doping out trends. We're working now five years ahead. Mr. Fruehauf'll get up to speak and maybe he stresses girls. Why? Well, because we don't know what's going to happen in 1955 and we can't be topical; but we know there'll always be girls, so at this get-together the eight hundred calendar people get a chance to hear a man like Mr. Fruehauf. You really ought to come out there for that get-together as a guest. You'd have yourself one hell of a time."

"Say, you forgot to tell the Prince about the art exhibition we have. Artists from all over the country compete in girl pictures."

"That's right," said Mr. Tannenbaum. "And Mr. Fruehauf here hands out the prizes to the artist that wins and to the girls that posed for the calendars. We — I mean Mr. Fruehauf — never does anything halfway."

Mr. Fruehauf's mind was far away now, at the get-together perhaps. He had anchored the cigar in his teeth, and his thumbs were stuck inside his loyalty belt.

He sank away in pleasant slumber. . . . It was an hour later that Mr. Tannenbaum woke us by moving his chair suddenly and jumping to his feet. He said a quick good-by.

Madame l'Ambassadrice was back. "Don't you think you should go up and take a rest, dear?" said the Ambassador, rising.

"Just to think of going up to that lousy room makes me feel like crying. I never did like French hotels anyway, or the French either, and now they're getting completely out of hand; even the croupiers. Imagine, one of them says to me *Décidez-vous* after I had put down my chips and said *Zéro Deux*. 'I have decided,' I said to him, 'I have decided that you are *un trei∂ mal elevay*' and I picked up my chips and went to another table. I tell you, they just sit around and expect us Americans to get them out of their troubles. Oh, Cucu, I'm so glad you're here. You know, *cheri,* you're the one exception I make."

The next day the morning sun stretched the shadow of

Signor Stuzzicadenti across the terrace and bent it up the side of the white hotel. He was talking to the Brazilian ladies who were enjoying the view from their deck chairs.

"What a lovely tree," said one of them, looking upward. It was a huge candelabra of a tree with a smooth bark that seemed to have been rubbed to an antique white by a decorator. The leaves seemed to have been placed carefully here and there, each one large, heart-shaped and pale green. The blossoms were as yet only half-open, and of delicate shining mother-of-pearl texture, tinted a pale violet at the base. The lukewarm wind moved among the branches and slowly tossed the leaves back and forth.

"When I was king . . ." said a slim man passing by to his companion.

His appearance electrified the old ladies. They looked at him with affectionate recognition; they seemed almost to curtsy as they lay in their deck chairs.

The rest of what the man said was lost in the droning roar of motors. Signor Stuzzicadenti did one of his lightning aboutfaces. He stamped his right foot on the marble floor of the terrace and, looking upward, allowed his furious gaze to follow the plane as it passed over the golden sign and above the branches of the tulip tree out into the blue Mediterranean sky.

12.

A Good Morning,
a Quiet Evening

"GOOD MORNING," said Signor Stuzzicadenti, simply and as to the wall, to Mr. Tannenbaum, who was taking an early walk. And then as it should be said—as if presenting arms—he sang, "*Bon jour, mon Prince, bon jour,* Monsieur le Comte." He smiled and rubbed his hands. "It is indeed a good morning for me—listen," he said, and turned his right ear upward, cupping it. With the other hand he pulled out his watch. It was nine, and there was no sound, except the raking of a gardener, and then a soft, faraway humming. Signor Stuzzicadenti smiled, his mouth

168

open all the way to his wisdom teeth. The beautiful Air France plane appeared far away, flying in a wide circle several kilometers distant. It sank to the field with no more noise than an eggbeater in a bowl of mayonnaise.

Signor Stuzzicadenti looked with happiness at his now perfect establishment.

"So you finally succeeded," said the doorman.

"Ah," said the Director, "not I, not the Ministry of Transport, not the Commissariat du Tourisme, but Madame l'Ambassadrice. What a woman! I am sorry to lose her. Madame and Monsieur l'Ambassadeur are leaving tonight. They are traveling in a private car, via Milano. One is always affected to see one's good guests leave; in this case I am profoundly sorry. Americans are the only kind of people to have these days — and I say that, believe me, in spite of my waiting list which is so long and distinguished that the manager of any hotel in France would gladly send me his fingers in the mail to obtain it. *Alors,* excuse me — " Having lost a good deal of time with us, he made two quick bows from the hip, executed an about-face and ran into his perfect hotel.

"That means I have a night off — because she'll be busy packing," said St. Cucuface. To make certain he called her on the phone and then he said, "We'll have a quiet evening by ourselves. We'll drive out to a little restaurant, have a good dinner and then come back and see her off on the train at midnight. After a day or so of swimming and a little sun we'll start off and drive back slowly over the Route Napoleon, a road as wild as anything in the Dakotas."

He remained in this sensible mood for at least an hour. He

watched the tennis games for a while, and then he went into the hotel and came back in a French bathing suit, too loose for him. Walking on the heels of his bare feet he passed over the wet mosaic that was laid about the pool, and then he cupped his hand, put one foot down into the water, wet himself and swam in an old-fashioned, frog-like breast stroke, *one, two, three,* up the pool. His swimming was so rhythmic that I said loudly, "*Eins, zwei, drei,*" without noticing it. I counted in German because I was taught to swim exactly like that, in a German school, by a drill-sergeant type of a screaming instructor who always counted, "*Eins, zwei, drei.*"

A man nearby smiled, and I told him how I came to count in German. He was very delicate, and looked like a pale Haile Selassie with a gray beard. He walked to me with mechanical motion. Although it was early morning he was dressed as if about to go for an audience with a ruling monarch. He stopped, clicked his heels and bowed. "*Bon jour, Monseigneur,*" he said, handing me an elegantly engraved card, on which was written "Aristide Trémouillas," and a number, and "Avenue de la Faisandrie, Paris." He transferred his gray gloves from his left hand to his right and raised his free hand, with bloodless fingers, the nails of which were like the scales of a small fish, to his gray beard, and took hold of it, in a manner that was like sticking a leaden paperclip to some papers. He seemed then to pull his mouth open with this heavy clip, and pensively he said in German, "*Ja ja-ja-ja.* The German language is good for counting strokes. I had a German instructor also in my childhood, and when he caned me he made me count—sometimes up to *dreizehn, vierzehn, fünfzehn*—and I've never forgotten it either."

Cucuface climbed up out of the water. He held his nose and

shivered, and he said, "This is suddenly like a week end in the country. Do you like week ends in the country?"

I said, "No."

"I can sleep in a railroad station," he said, "or in the Metro, but barnyard noises, the crowing of roosters and the raking of gravel in the morning, such things drive me mad. I can't stand this." He dried his thin legs. "Is there anything more tiresome than people lying about in the sun?" he said, and dressed in a hurry. In the lobby he approached the Director.

"What I want," said St. Cucuface, "is a ticket of admission to the Casino for my friend here, the Prince de Bavière. He and I are leaving tomorrow and he wants to see the inside of the Casino. He has never been in such a place. I have a season card and I will sponsor him."

"Consider it arranged," said Signor Stuzzicadenti.

"I feel better now," said Cucuface.

HIS WHOLE BEING had changed, as if he had taken a strong drug. He walked faster and he stood straighter. His hands were active; he rubbed them together, clasped and unclasped them. He picked up several chairs and moved them around as he walked about. He pulled back his cuffs and was as nervous as Signor Stuzzicadenti.

"I will tell you something," he said. "Up in my room, at the bottom of my bag, is my good-luck garment, a dirty old sweater. It is much darned and it has never been washed or dry cleaned, because I must preserve its magic. I have never worn it when I went gambling with Madame l'Ambassadrice and that is why we consistently lost. I did not feel that I should wear it, I was not really playing. I was merely putting a little money on this and on that and it didn't matter. Now it matters." He gripped the back of another chair as he continued his intense talk.

"That old sweater—for years it has protected me like a cloak made of all the medals of all the saints in Paradise. Once when I had inherited—and received—two million dollars, *dollars*, mind you, not francs, I immediately bought myself the latest and largest Rolls-Royce obtainable, and then of course took it for a drive in the country. After a long evening of card-playing and celebrating, I drove home. Being a cosmopolitan, and finding myself in a new English car with the steering wheel on the right side, I drove as I would in England, on the left side, and at a furious clip. I had a terrible head-on collision in the Champs Élysées with a statue of Clemenceau, which I hit trying to avoid an oncoming lorry. It knocked Monsieur Clemenceau off his pedestal but nothing happened to me, and I know why— because coming back from a poker game, with my winnings in my pockets, I still wore the lucky sweater. Since then it has always brought me luck. I know exactly when to wear it. It has had a long rest; I will wear it tonight. I don't want any lunch. I'm going to the Casino to test the air—as one might say—to walk the track as one does before driving in an auto race, to see where the soft spots are, to judge the climate. It helps a lot.

"In the beginning, I went with Madame l'Ambassadrice; she brings bad luck, and I didn't like the croupiers at all. They're new here; this Casino has been open for only twenty years, and in that little time, it is impossible to make a good croupier. In Monte Carlo it is in the blood, the grandfather was a croupier; you sense it immediately."

He came back in the late afternoon. He usually drank champagne instead of cocktails, and the waiter came with a napkin-wrapped ice bottle of his favorite kind. St. Cucuface held up his hands and said: "Give me twice nothing," which is the French equivalent of "Pour me just a drop."

He seemed unable to keep his mind on anything; he was twitchy and nervous and he made faces that I had never seen on him before.

During the coffee, the Director brought my card of admission. He asked us whether we had seen in the papers that a ring of crooks working apparently with someone on the inside had succeeded in playing with marked cards. They were extremely clever, they used especial eyeglasses. These glasses were so conditioned that only with them a certain marking was visible. St. Cucuface bit his fingernails and stared bleakly out at the tulip tree. He had not heard a word of what the Director had said.

An elegant, sharp, middle-aged American, who seemed to be engaged in various businesses, came up and said to St. Cucuface: "I've got something for you, something very interesting. Mumpitz Keregowitch is leaving suddenly. He's been living on his yacht, the *Esmeralda*, down there at the dock with six Greeks, all of them gamblers, and they're washed up. You can buy the boat for next to nothing, use it for the rest of the season and sell it next year for double what you pay. It's the best buy on the coast. She was built in Kiel and there's also an Alfa Romeo goes with it. It's brand new and they're selling it for half."

"Will you please go away," said St. Cucuface, and closed his eyes.

The American put his hands in his pockets, shrugged, and walked away as though there had been no conversation.

St. Cucuface asked the waiter for pencil and paper and began to make notations.

He muttered to himself, and apparently agreed completely with what he said, for he nodded and smiled bitterly. He still looked worried and doubtful when I left the table to go to look down at the yacht which was for sale.

"If the dames they have on board go with it, I'll buy it. Ha ha ha ha—" said a fat little man to the American.

"Oh, don't worry, they go with it all right. For that matter, I could find you even better," said the agent.

"I'd be satisfied with what's there. How much do you think—"

"Make me an offer."

I went back to the table. St. Cucuface looked up from his paper, and gazed at me with surprise.

"Oh," he said, "It's you. Now don't worry. We're going to be all right tonight."

He disappeared for the rest of the afternoon, but was as restless during dinner as he had been at lunch and he drank nothing.

"We begin at nine o'clock," he said and went upstairs. He undressed and put on the dirty sweater next to his skin, then the stiff-bosomed evening shirt over it. He turned to me and said abruptly, "You've got to be on guard. One thing we have to watch out for—if I shouldn't notice it when we're at the tables, look for three women walking into the room together, for me— that's fatal. If that happens we stop playing at once. However, it is very good to have a man with a beard next to us. It is also bad if three women walk into the room one after the other; watch out for that, too; but that is not as bad as three together."

We went to Cannes. Its eccentric houses, villas and toy palaces are nearly all built for pleasure; one could place the Pyramids, the Taj Mahal and Grant's Tomb into the center of it and they would scarcely be noticed. Past the names of a hundred *pensions* and hotels that stand balcony to balcony, we came down to the old harbor by way of the Quai St. Pierre and walked along the Promenade. Turn left and there is the Casino Municipal. Up the stairs and through the door and one comes to an immense outer hall that is nearly square. In the center, like a cork bobbing up and down in the ocean, a violinist led an orchestra of ten pieces that played for three waiters and one hundred and twenty-eight little glass-topped tables, each with four small golden chairs. On each table stood an ashtray, on each fifth table was a highball glass filled with straws, and the shiny dance floor lay quietly in the center.

An old man in heavy livery, with silver-buckled leather pumps on his flat feet, marched ahead of us. It was like a funeral without a corpse. Adjusting our pace to his, we followed the gold-braided guardian down to the left, then made a sharp turn to the right, then left again. St. Cucuface became very tense and began to sniff the air. We heard the small clicking-chip sounds of the gambling room inside. There were two men at the door, not the anthropoid types that guard the doors of most New York night clubs, but nice men, such as one would find taking up collections in church. Here all is done with nods and whispers and discreet smiles. The two deacons bowed us inside and we came to a small bank where another ascetic counted chips and money with a magician's swift, flowing dexterity.

St. Cucuface said: "Let me play for you. We will go fifty-fifty.

And we will invest a thousand dollars to start with." He looked at me and said, "Well, five hundred then."

He was now laced tight with tenseness. I watched the door: one woman, a very old one, came in, but she was followed by a man. St. Cucuface's mouth was drawn thin as a turtle's; his eyes were burning and he even seemed to have lost some of his hair since morning; he seemed thinner—he seemed to be someone else.

There were the tables, as one expected them to be, and everything looked the way it does in the films. The people who sat around the tables were the ones who sit around the tables in the movies: little old ghosts of women playing, their elaborate bookkeeping in front of them, in a corner a collection of intent faces, pale with avarice—the owner of one of them was losing heavily but kept calmly replacing his bets with larger sums. I noted that the Haile Selassie type with the beard was playing near the end of the table.

St. Cucuface bought his chips, and separated them into piles of ten, each representing about a hundred dollars. He went first to the table at the right. There are at each side of the roulette two fields that one may play; and away from the fields, further down on the cloth to the left and right, are three squares, each bearing the number twelve. St. Cucuface suddenly placed his chips on one of the twelves. The warning came that no more bets would be accepted, the little ball started rolling, and St. Cucuface had won. He repeated the maneuver and won again. In ten minutes, always playing the three twelves, he had so many chips that he had difficulty in holding them. He went back to the bank and changed them into oval chips, each

representing three hundred dollars. He now played two tables simultaneously, going from one to the other to pick up his winnings. Apparently it was a common occurrence. The other players and the croupiers paid not the slightest attention. In general, however, a great deal more money was being raked in than was being paid out. He lost twice in a row at large stakes.

St. Cucuface had become a creature of nervous hands, feet and burning eyes; his face was gray and haggard. The pile of chips had become awkwardly large again. He cashed them in, stuffed the money into his pocket. He had discarded whatever system he had plotted and stuck to betting this twelve or that twelve, or two twelves astride. It worked most times.

I have never won anything in my life and gambling has never interested me. I stood there and looked at what St. Cucuface was doing on the other side of the table. It seemed monotonously easy. I got some chips for myself and went to the other end of the table. Again he placed about a thousand dollars' worth of chips on the rightmost twelve. I did the same thing; the breathless moment came —*phrrrrr* went the little ivory pellet— and I had tripled my stake. It happened again and again. Now my pockets were heavy and I went back to change the chips into the oval ones. After three more plays, Cucuface suddenly stopped. Three women had entered the room, Indian file. He looked at me reproachfully. "You didn't watch. Now we'll have to wait."

We watched other players for a while, cashed in some chips and then, as if he had received some ghostly remote instructions, Cucuface was back again. He played at both tables, the left twelve, and doubled, the left twelve again and doubled, the left twelve once more, the left twelve once again, and still another time. And then he stopped.

"The man with the beard is leaving. Let us eat," he said.

He put some money on the table for the employees, each of whom thanked him politely, as with the rake the gift was stuffed into a kind of letter-drop built into the table. We cashed in all our chips. French money is very beautiful and it is as feather-light as the frailest air-mail stationery. We had accumulated so much that it weighed us down and filled all the pockets of our coats and trousers.

The restaurant at the Casino Municipal is exquisite in appointments, food and service. The passion for gambling exhausts, and Cucuface's limbs hung from his torso like a puppet's, his eyelids were heavy and he was very pale. At a table nearby the man with the beard was eating barley soup and drinking milk.

"It's the worst thing for you, even as an aphrodisiac the common shrimp or celery root is better, but here they have really good caviar, so let's order some," said Cucuface.

They brought it in those large blue cans and they didn't measure it out with a small spoon. They put the onions and the eggs, the little pancakes and the toast at the table and one helped oneself. Onion and eggs can spoil caviar when it is first-rate, and so we ate it plain, great full plates of it, we ate it as if it were porridge and washed it down with the superb champagne.

"I am too tired to count this money," said St. Cucuface. "We'll leave most of it at the desk and then we will go back. What do you think of my dirty little old sweater now?"

St. Cucuface drank the iced champagne as if it were water.

On his cheeks two crimson spots appeared, his eyes were feverish bright again, and his face twitched.

The old gentleman looked up from his table, and took hold of his gray beard, and stroked it, and then he carefully added the bill, and slowly paid out an obligatory amount for the waiter. He looked across at us, and St. Cucuface asked him if his losses had been great.

"Oh, no," said Monsieur Trémouillas. "On the contrary." He looked like a mystery man.

"You have a system?" asked Cucuface.

"It's not exactly a system—it's the only way you consistently can make money—you can even support yourself that way. I do," said Monsieur Trémouillas.

"Would you mind telling me, is it complicated?" asked the count.

"Simplicity itself," said the mystery man. "You limit yourself to what you can afford to lose a day—with me it is a thousand francs. When that is gone, I stop. When I win it goes into another pocket. I consistently win enough over a period of a month to take care of my simple needs." With that Monsieur Trémouillas got up. He walked with us to the door of the gaming rooms. The two young men there asked us for our cards.

"Oh," said the little man, and bowing correctly he backed away from us.

As we were about to enter the gaming rooms, one of the ascetic young men asked us to follow him; he had a little matter he wanted to talk to us about, he said. He led the way to a side room where there were two gentlemen from the police.

"I must ask for your cards of admission," said the nice young man, and when we gave them to him, he put them into his pocket.

"I am very sorry," he said to St. Cucuface. "You are of course known here, but you have introduced this gentleman with you and have thereby violated paragraph so and so, of the club charter."

"I beg your pardon?" said St. Cucuface.

"The Commissaire of the police will explain," said the polite young man and took himself out of hearing with very precise steps.

One policeman remained near the door. The other came over and bowed and said to me: "You are His Highness, the Prince de Bavière, at least that is how you have registered here. May I ask Your Highness to allow me to have a look at your papers? Your passport, if you please?"

"Sorry, but I don't have it with me."

"Where is it, Your Highness?"

"At my hotel—"

The policeman smiled at me benignly:

"I regret, *alors*, that we must accompany you there—"

St. Cucuface said coldly: "This gentleman is my friend. He is not, *alors*, the Prince de Bavière, but he is an American citizen. *Alors*, it was a joke—"

"Ah, messieurs, but jokes like this sometimes end very badly. Now I think we shall have to accompany you to the Commissariat."

The Commissariat in Cannes was infested by the same smells as those in Paris. It was as badly lighted, and behind the desk sat exactly the same kind of commissaire.

St. Cucuface talked to him very earnestly, and the Commissaire picked up the phone and called Signor Stuzzicadenti, who fell over himself. We had to wait until a boy appeared with my passport, with explanations.

The Commissaire said that as one who was run ragged by jewel thieves, robbers, swindlers, and international confidence men, he was relieved that we offered so simple a problem. Since the Casino had not lodged a complaint, and since I was, *alors*, not a prince but an American, we were free to go.

"Of course, you may not go back to play tonight. The Casino will not readmit you," said the Commissaire. "Tomorrow, if you choose to come as yourself, properly identified, that of course will be another matter."

The Commissaire got up and accepted a cigarette out of the golden case of the count. As we went into the hall two policemen brought in Monsieur Trémouillas. "Oh, it's you," said the Commissaire as to an old client.

Cucuface said, "I'll never win anything again in my whole life if I don't get the gray beard out." With that he went back into the office. In a little while the Haile Selassie type came out with the same two policemen and ran away up the street, pushing along with his black cane and disappearing around the corner as if the wind were pulling him.

"Just an ordinary kind of impostor," said Cucuface. "I wasted my time going back. He got himself free; he knows the law better than the *Juge d'Instruction.*"

Monsieur Trémouillas operated, the Commissaire explained, "to the prejudice of the naïve." He was a common impostor, who thanks to an ingenious strategy of *escroquerie* managed to stay in the best hotels, dress impeccably and travel a good deal.

"He does it all with paper," said the Commissaire. "The impressive stationery of Monsieur Trémouillas is sent out on the occasion of appointments to high ministerial posts, to congratulate a man of affairs on the marriage of his daughter, his appointment to the Tribunal of the Seine, or the French Academy, the awarding of decorations and orders. Of course these people answer on equally important papers; their secretaries compose excessive formulas of politeness and gratitude and assurances of esteem and respect. Under these letters are placed the most distinguished autographs. The letters are then carefully preserved, and with their aid Monsieur Aristide Trémouillas creates an aura of importance, the illusion of being at home in the most inaccessible foyers in France. His game is to intervene in various matters, furthering projects, getting priorities and creating a favorable climate. He most cleverly jockeys his victims into a position in which they offer him money. He never asks for it. His income, he says, comes from the Casino and a system that he follows—a system that requires iron discipline. *Alors*, messieurs, I have been in Cannes for years—it is possible that a man can go to the tables and win a lot of money, but he must take the train and never come back again. Return and you lose it. Nobody makes money at gambling but the Casino, not even this Monsieur Trémouillas. The most we can do is to ask him to move, because his papers are not altogether in order. He has a restricted passport—he enjoys political asylum in France—of course his name is not Trémouillas."

St. Cucuface pressed some of the beautiful air-mail currency on both the policemen who had brought us when we finally left the Commissariat. He asked them for a place that had *ambiance*.

Ambiance is a word that should be taken over into English, it means "a happy mood."

The policemen directed us to a Hungarian place. On the way there we heard the shrill high whistle of a train.

"We must not forget Madame l'Ambassadrice," said St. Cucuface.

The Restaurant Budapest had carpets nailed to the walls, to the ceiling and on the floor. There was drapery, and oriental lamps, and three glowing blonde girls with snow-white blouses and marzipan-colored flesh bulging under and above the linen. Two had eyes like synthetic jewels—the first, immense emeralds, the second, sapphires—while those of the third were a soft brown, the exact hue of horse chestnuts when children in a park peel them and they emerge moist and polished from their white soft shells. They seemed as ardent in their behavior as they were in appearance.

"We are fortunate," said St. Cucuface. "You know we owe it all to my dirty little sweater. It was the sweater that brought the police, without the police we would have gone back again, and I am not certain that would have been a good thing. I have often observed it: unless you are thrown out, you lose it all. Anyway, here we are."

"What you will have," asked the one with the horse-chestnut eyes.

The violinist bent low over his instrument and the gypsy orchestra began to play softly.

"Champagne," said St. Cucuface and selected the wine.

"Curious, isn't it, that Hungary produces the gayest and most beautiful of women, and at the same time, the ugliest men," he said.

The orchestra consisted of five men. Each looked as if he were wearing someone else's head. There was an oversize skull on the cellist, whose face looked like a Beethoven death mask done by an amateur. The violinist had a nose like a calabash, the cymbalist's face was a folded concertina—all of them had dark, pock-marked masklike faces and they made the very best gypsy music.

St. Cucuface had made his transition into the third mood: he put his arms around the sapphire-eyed girl, who had hips like a Percheron; he gave her a handful of money and ordered her to serve a quart of champagne to each of the musicians. The one with the green eyes was sent to the telephone to order a ten-pound can of caviar to be brought from the Casino, and the third, the one with the chestnut eyes, he simply asked to sit down and hold his hand. St. Cucuface was sad.

"*Wenn der Ungar lustig ist—muss er immer weinen,*" said the girl with the brown eyes.

"Ah, what does it mean?" said St. Cucuface. "When the Hungarian is happy, he must weep." He sighed with a sound like the sea before a storm. "Play, Gypsy!" he yelled.

The musicians came up and they played so close to us that it was as if we had the instruments in our hands.

St. Cucuface stuffed money under the bridges of the fiddles, into the double bass, and into the vest of the ecstatic cymbalist.

The caviar came, and was served. We were the only customers in the place.

The *ambiance* continued to increase as the three girls, the five musicians, the doorman who had been called in from the street and the father of the girls, who was also the proprietor, all joined in the party, singing, dancing, playing music and eating caviar.

St. Cucuface, very soberly, asked for the time and suddenly announced that he was sick of Cannes. "L'Ambassadrice has enough room on the train—for us," he said. The brown-eyed daughter was instructed to call Signor Stuzzicadenti and to tell him to have our things packed and sent to the train. After another half hour of the greatest gaiety, St. Cucuface announced that the entire personnel of the Restaurant Budapest would go to see us depart.

He made detailed plans for provisioning the train: the doorman was to ice the bottles and procure the Ambassador's favorite whiskey. In four taxis the wine and the music rolled down to the station. The cymbalist had exchanged his instrument for a guitar. After St. Cucuface had arranged for their entry to the train platform, the gypsies preceded us to the compartment of Madame l'Ambassadrice.

Since there are no private cars in Europe, except those belonging to Dictators and the President of France, Madame l'Ambassadrice had engaged an entire *wagon-lit*. The doors of the various compartments had been opened, giving the party the spaciousness of several sets of double rooms.

The Ambassadress achieved immediately the *ambiance* of the party. Undamaged by the passage through the dark streets, the mood had been moved to the car.

The corks popped, the Ambassador was pleased with his whiskey and especially with the girls, all of whom had great calendar possibilities. The orchestra had been installed and the faces of the passengers and those who had come to see them off were all very happy, for nowhere else in the world is pleasure a thing so agreed upon as in France.

The conductor of the train arrived with the porter of the

sleeping car, and announced that the train was about to depart. The proprietor of the Restaurant Budapest pushed his daughters along the corridor and herded them down the steps. St. Cucuface informed the musicians: "You are to remain; you are to travel with us," and ordered the conductor to open more wine for the musicians. They held out their glasses as they stood with their hats and coats on, and were beginning to bow and say good night when St. Cucuface gave each one another handful of money and told them to take off their hats and coats and continue playing. "Get off one station before the border," said St. Cucuface, "and hire a car to drive you back. I will pay for it."

Madame l'Ambassadrice said, "Oh, Cucu, how brilliant of you not to let them go! Now we can have a real party. And look what Stuzzi did for me — dear Stuzzi — he almost wept when we left." Signor Stuzzicadenti had sent an immense basket of roses and a veritable buffet of delicacies. At that moment the train started and Madame l'Ambassadrice fell into St. Cucuface's arms. The musicians played ardently. "Isn't it fun, Cucu, oh, isn't it wonderful to have *friends!*" cried Madame l'Ambassadrice. In the corridor toward the end of the car, the outcast Mr. Tannenbaum was smoking a cigar and the cold night air pulled its smoke around him like a wreath and spiralled it out of the window.

The music had adapted its rhythm to that of the train, and each of the Hungarians had a fresh bottle of champagne. There was a delay of more than an hour in Nice, and the *ambiance* was no longer in the same evidence. The Ambassador was sleepy; Mr. Tannenbaum had turned in. The Beethoven cellist yawned, the music played softly out of consideration for the passengers in the adjoining cars, and then, like a sigh, it ceased altogether.

Madame l'Ambassadrice had disappeared. St. Cucuface asked for his compartment, and I went to mine. There is nothing so thorough as the service of a truly first-class train in France. Toilet articles had been put into the proper places, pajamas laid out, the light adjusted, the bed turned down, the slippers in place, and there were farewell gifts for each one of his departing guests with the card of Signor Stuzzicadenti: two golden dice in a jewelers' box. I sleep easily on any train. After an hour or so of rolling through a Riviera dawn there was a stop and a burst of conversation outside in the corridor, and St. Cucuface came into my compartment. He was wearing a black overcoat over his pajamas and he said that something bothersome had occurred.

St. Cucuface in his exuberance had not noticed that the train was departing in the wrong direction. When I inquired of the conductor in some alarm, I was informed that on account of a earthslide, the Paris express was being rerouted. The Hungarians had overslept and had neglected to disembark and now we were in Italy and none of them, it appeared, had any papers. What was worse, the leader had confessed to him that they were illegally in France. The conductor was called, and with him came the French Customs official and the Italian Passport Control. We went back to see the Hungarians, and if ordinary people can look sad in such circumstances, the Hungarians did infinitely better. It was, besides, the very worst *ambiance* — the *ambiance* of awakening in the early morning after too little sleep, of railroad station, of hopelessness and officialdom.

"Let me speak to them," said the conductor. He took the customs and passport men with him into the now abandoned compartment where the departure had been celebrated.

St. Cucuface joined the officials and returned to say: "Luck-ily we have all that money. Give me a hundred thousand francs, because for that sum the officials will become suddenly blind as far as the Hungarians are concerned. They have already agreed to this solution." As the train jerked into motion, St. Cucuface said: "But you must let them off." "Let who off?" said the passport *contrôleur* as he stepped down from the moving train. "It's all right," said the Italian conductor, "just tell them to be quiet and everything will be all right."

"But this train is going to Switzerland—"

"To Switzerland? No, it is going to Genoa—"

"The car is going to Berne—"

"Oh," said the official, "I am very sorry."

St. Cucuface called for the conductor again. "What will we do with these Hungarians?" he asked. "When we get to Switzerland—"

"Ah, that is difficult," said the conductor. "We should have let them off at the French border. One can always arrange oneself with the Italians and the French, but the Swiss have no sense of humor, and they are without imagination. You can offer them money; they want it, they may need it, but they will not take it."

The Hungarians, looking like a cabinet of horrors, sat sur-rounded by their instruments, staring bleakly into space. None of them, it seemed, had any suggestions to make.

Mr. Tannenbaum was up with the first light of day and fully dressed. He stood in the corridor and his cigar smoke whip-lashed about in the draft. He was also of no help.

Madame l'Ambassadrice arose at ten and came into the salon. She had a morning hair-do; it looked like golden caracul fur. Madame was wearing her morning jewels and was delighted to hear that the Hungarians were still aboard. "We'll have them for dinner," she said. St. Cucuface sat about and worried. The Hungarians were still in a state of paralysis. In the daylight, their faces were a greenish gray, the yellow of their eyes was bloodshot and in this light also the tailcoat of the leader and the dinner jackets and trousers of the others were seen to be frayed and stained. The funeral *ambiance* increased as the train approached the Swiss border.

Madame's maid brought a tooled box which contained what seemed to be a game but was a Hérmes seating kit, consisting of a central ivory piece which represented the table. This could be made long, square, round or oval, and there were pegs to which cards were attached and one could plan the seating arrangement for a meal that way. Madame was busy seating a dinner for a while. She had her golden pencil and she looked out of the window and then scratched her head with the pencil. Then she looked at St. Cucuface and said, "What's the matter with you?" He explained.

"Why in heaven's name didn't you tell me, Cucu?" she said. "What in hell have we got an Ambassador on board for?" She sent for him and gave him his orders. At first he looked bewildered; and then he made a face.

"If anybody says anything to anybody about this, they're a delegation to the UN. They by God certainly look it," said Madame l'Ambassadrice. "And you're not to be disturbed." The Ambassador wondered whether he had that much authority.

"You know, dear," he said mildly, "the Swiss don't get any Marshall aid. They've got about as much dough as anybody. They're independent."

Madame l'Ambassadrice said, "Listen, will you do as I tell you?"

"Very well," said the Ambassador glumly. "Tell Tannenbaum I want to see him."

"Isn't it wonderful," said St. Cucuface, "that a woman like Madame l'Ambassadrice, who is not only beautiful and intelligent not to say intellectual, has, besides all her other qualities, also those of a diplomat."

With the aid of Mr. Tannenbaum, a conference was arranged. The Hungarians sat around a table and were given cigars and drinks, and a sign was hung on the door. When the passport people came, Tannenbaum called the Ambassador out and he was saluted and believed and the train rumbled unmolested through Switzerland and back into France, where St. Cucuface paid the Hungarians once more. They were now deliriously happy, showing their various sets of bad, tobacco-stained and gold-capped teeth as they smiled. They obliged with a final concert. On the way from the train, we saw two of them, like shabby shadows, crossing the Place Vendôme.

IT IS IMPOSSIBLE, once you have it, to shake off an incognito.

I had returned to the bourgeois safety of the old Hôtel St. Julien le Pauvre, and taken up again the fight with the French telephone, and patiently I underwent the daily beating handed to the tourist.

Once Cucuface came, and he pulled a golden cigarette case

from his coat pocket. I was prepared to buy it from him, but it was not his own.

"It's for you—from Madame l'Ambassadrice. She had it made for the pleasure of dictating to a jeweler: 'To my dear friend, the Prince de Bavière.'"

It had a large crest on the outside, and a crown on its back, and the dedication was engraved on the inside. I accepted it as a souvenir and I'm thinking of selling it to Cucuface—or at least I will try to lose it.

A while ago I had to go to Lisbon, and there is an excellent restaurant run by Germans, called Horcher. Sitting there I saw opposite me the bearded Haile Selassie type. He looked at me and he couldn't place me. I said across the room to him, "*Eins, zwei, drei.*"

"*Ja ja-ja-ja, eins, zwei,*" he answered as to a secret code.

With the coffee I pulled my cigarette case out, and as I took a cigarette from it the *Oberkellner* of that restaurant (that is, the maître d'hôtel) observed the crest, and, being properly trained as German *Oberkellners* of the old school are, he pulled himself together and said, "*Wünschen Königliche Hoheit einen Branntwein?*" which means "Does Your Royal Highness desire any brandy?" In the gracious tone of a monseigneur I said no. He removed himself walking backwards, and he attended to the needs of the gray beard across the room, and they talked in German. The *Oberkellner's* face changed as he looked across at me. I am sure that the gray beard had said to him, "*Passen Sie auf—dieser Mann da drüben ist ein Hochstapler,*" which means "Beware, that man across there is an impostor."

Books Forming a Series
By and About Ludwig Bemelmans

NOVELS

Father, Dear Father (1992)
    by Ludwig Bemelmans (0-87008-136-5)

I Love You, I Love You, I Love You (1992)
    by Ludwig Bemelmans (0-87008-137-3)

How to Travel Incognito (1992)
    By Ludwig Bemelmans (0-87008-138-1)

BIBLIOGRAPHY

Ludwig Bemelmans: A Comprehensive Bibliography (1992)
    edited by Murray Pommerance (0-87008-140-3)

Other Titles in Preparation

Louis Bemelmans [signature]

Bemelmans tales overflow with whimsical eccentrics, somber head waiters, and a long string of charmingly irresponsible and wholly unlikely people and situations. The plots of his stories lead to improbable solutions. We journey with him through western Europe and Latin America, and we learn first hand from this master writer and illustrator of exisiting warmth in people and places. His exuberance for life and humanity creates nostalgia, a fresh glow and a yearning for more of the same. His writings and book illustrations brim over with light-hearted satire and joyful humor. In short, Bemelmans makes us feel good.

This book was composed in
Cochin and Nicholas Cochin Black
by The Sarabande Press, New York.

It was printed and bound by
Arcata Graphics Company, New York
on 60# Sebago cream white antique paper.

The typography and binding were designed by
Beth Tondreau Design, New York.